Also by Sylvia Day

HEAT OF THE NIGHT
PLEASURES OF THE NIGHT

Spellbound

SYLVIA DAY

wm

WILLIAM MORROW
An Imprint of HarperCollinsPublishers

FIRST EDITION

Designed by Diahann Sturge

Library of Congress Cataloging-in-Publication Data has been applied for.

ISBN 978-0-06-230549-7

13 14 15 16 17 DIX/RRD 10 9 8 7 6 5 4 3 2 1

Contents

Spellbound

A Familiar Kind of Magic

One

The Hunter had finally arrived.

Victoria studied him carefully through the closed-circuit feed that monitored her office reception area. The urbane Armani suit he wore did nothing to hide the predator within. Tall and dark, the Hunter moved with a casual arrogance that made her purr. He didn't look around, completely focused on the moment when they would be together in the same room. Alone.

As she rubbed her hands together, a throaty growl filled the air. The High Council was ready to tangle with her again. She smiled and preened, as was the nature of her kind. This Hunter was powerful, she could feel it even through the walls that separated them.

It was a testament to her own prowess that They would send a warlock such as him after her. She couldn't help but be flattered. After all, she'd broken the laws on purpose, deliberately goading the very powers that had stolen Darius from her. And here was her "punishment," walking into her office with that luscious, long-legged stride. She couldn't be more thrilled with their choice.

He flashed a devastating smile at the receptionist before she closed the door behind him. Then he turned his attention to Victoria and removed his sunglasses.

Oh my.

She crossed her silk-stocking clad legs to ease the sudden ache between them.

Piercing gray eyes measured her from a face so austerely handsome she was almost inclined to leave her seat and rub up against him. *That firm jaw ... those sculpted lips ...*

But, of course, she couldn't. She first had to see if he would reveal who he was or if he intended to pretend. The High Council still hadn't realized how much power Darius had bequeathed her. They didn't yet realize how deeply her awareness went.

Her gaze moved to the crystal-framed miniature on her desk and the man with the rakish dimple who smiled lovingly from there. Captured beautifully in oil paints, glints of gold shining in his blond hair, the sight of Darius brought a familiar ache of loss and heartache that firmed her resolve. The waste of his life filled her with a need for retribution.

Rising to her feet, Victoria held out her hand. The Hunter took it leisurely, the palpable force in his touch betraying him.

"Mr. Westin," she breathed, fighting back a delicious shiver. She would have to thank the Council for this gift when she was done with him. He was so dark—his skin, his raven hair, his aura. Sex incarnate. She could smell it, feel it with his proximity. It was obvious why he was a successful Hunter. Already she was wet and eager.

Max Westin held her hand a little too long, his thickly lashed gaze clearly stating his intentions to have her, to tame her. Like all kittens, Victoria liked to play, so she brushed her fingertips across his palm as she pulled away. His eyes widened almost imperceptibly, a tiny sign that she could get to him if she really put the effort into it.

Of course, she intended to do just that. The Council only sent Their best, most prized Hunters after her, and she knew how it chaffed Them when Their elite met with abject failure. It was the only thing she could do to prevent feeling helpless—give Them a harsh reminder of how great Darius had been, and what They'd lost with his needless sacrifice.

"Ms. St. John." Westin's voice was a rough caress. Everything about him was a little rough, a little gritty. A primitive creature. Just like she was.

Victoria waved toward the chair in front of her glass-topped desk. Freeing the button of his coat, Max sank into the seat, his dark blue trousers stretching over firm thighs and an impressive bulge between them.

She licked her lips. *Yum . . .*

One side of his mouth curved in a knowing smile. Max Westin was well aware of how irresistible he was, which made him irresistible to her. Confidence was a quality she held in high esteem. So was a touch of wickedness, and Westin definitely had that. That dark aura betrayed the edges of black magic he skirted. She doubted the Council had any better leash on him than They had on her.

Liking him immensely already, Victoria sank into her own

chair, arranging her legs beneath her black pencil skirt to show them to best advantage.

"The museum offers its sincere apologies for the loss of your necklace," he began.

Her smile widened. He wasn't going to tell her who he was. *How delicious.* "You don't look like the curator type to me, Mr. Westin."

"I'm here on behalf of the museum's insurance company. Obviously a loss of this magnitude requires an investigation."

"That's reassuring, of course."

Observing him through the veil of her lashes, Victoria noted the energy that betrayed his restless nature. His firm, full lips hinted at sinful delights. She liked sinful, energetic men. This one was a bit rigid for her tastes, but that could change with the right persuasion. They all succumbed eventually. It was the only part of the game that disappointed her—the surrender.

"You seem remarkably at ease," Westin murmured, "for a woman who's just lost a priceless piece of jewelry."

Victoria's toes curled. His voice was so deep and slightly husky, like he just rolled out of bed. It was scrumptious, like the rest of him. He was so broad shouldered, yet lean, every movement he made a graceful ripple of honed muscle.

"Fretting won't accomplish anything," she said with a careless shrug. "Besides, you are here to find the necklace and you look . . . capable. What is there to worry about?"

"That I won't recover it. Your trust in my abilities is flattering, Ms. St. John, and not misplaced. I'm very good at what I do. However, sometimes things are not what they seem."

It was a warning, plain and simple.

Thoughtful, she stood and walked to the wall of windows

behind her desk. Despite having her back to him, Victoria felt the heat of his gaze caressing the length of her. She fingered the pearls that graced her neck and stared out over the city skyline. "If need be, I'll simply acquire another. Everything can be purchased for a price, Mr. Westin."

"Not everything."

Intrigued, Victoria turned, surprised to find him approaching. He took a position next to her, his gaze on the view, but his attention fully focused on her. She felt the shimmer of his power sweep over her, searching for her weaknesses.

Unable to resist the danger, she rubbed her shoulder against him and inhaled the rich, masculine scent of his skin—a mixture of thousand-dollar cologne and pure Max Westin. Her breathing became shallow, her heart rate picked up. Losing her perspective, Victoria moved away. It had been a long time since she'd indulged in a powerful man. Too long. The other Hunters had been crafty and seductive. Westin had that and pure magical muscle.

"Max," she called softly, hurrying their familiarity by using his first name.

"Hmm?"

She looked over her shoulder. He was following her. Stalking her. Reminding her that he was the predator here.

Oh, he could be fun. If he wanted to play.

"Have dinner with me."

"My place," he agreed.

She moved to the wet bar and retrieved two glass bottles of milk, a deliberate choice that showed her cognizance. Certainly he knew how she worked. But did he know why?

Did Westin know that with Darius's dying breath he had

transferred his magic to her, making her far more powerful than the average Familiar? Did Westin know that she'd been loved by her warlock, and that it was that love which gave her the ability to make her own choices now?

Before Darius's gift, she had been like other Familiars. The High Council assigned the pairings between her kind and their magical counterparts, regardless of their wishes. Some Familiars were unhappy with their partners. She had been lucky the first time, finding a love for Darius that transcended time. Now, because of that love, she was too powerful to be taken against her will. In the two centuries since she'd lost him, no other warlock had succeeded in collaring her. Westin would fare no better. She had loved once, and deeply. There would never be another warlock for her.

Swaying her hips and offering a seductive smile, she returned to him. "How about my place?"

"No." He took the bottle from her outstretched hand, his fingers deliberately curling over hers and staying there. Pinning her in place. "Victoria."

Her name, just one word, but spoken with such possession she could almost feel the collar around her neck. Hunters did not keep Familiars, they caught them and passed them on to lesser warlocks. She would never allow herself to be distributed in that manner again.

So they stood, touching, sizing each other up. She tilted her head and allowed her interest to show, not that she could hide it with her nipples hard and obvious beneath her green silk shirt. Her chest rose and fell with near panting breaths, her blood heating from both his proximity and his darkly seductive scent. He was so tall, so hard, so intense. Only the silky lock of dark hair that draped his brow softened his purely masculine features. If he weren't a Hunter, she'd be crawling all over him, she wanted him that badly.

As his gaze dropped to the swell of her breasts, his mouth curved in a carnal smile. "I bet I'm the better cook," he rasped softly, his fingers stroking hers, sending sparks of awareness through her.

She pouted. "You won't know if you don't come over."

He pulled away, his charm vanishing in an instant. "My place or I'll have to decline."

Victoria wished she were in her feline form so she could flick her tail at him. Max Westin was most definitely accustomed to getting what he wanted. He was a Dominant, as were all Hunters. Too bad she was, too.

"A pity." And she meant it, her disappointment was painful. His place was not an option. Who knew what spells he'd cast there? And what toys he had . . . ? It would be akin to walking into a cage.

She ignored the thrill the thought gave her.

"You changed your mind?" His surprise was a tangible thing.

The man definitely didn't hear "no" often enough.

"I asked you to dinner, Mr. Westin, and you placed restrictions on the invitation." She waved her hand toward the door in a gesture of dismissal designed to rile him. "I don't tolerate restrictions."

A return warning to him.

When he made no move to leave, she purred aloud, a soft rumbling sound that made the muscle in his jaw tic.

So . . . the raging attraction was reciprocated. That made her feel slightly better about waiting longer to have him.

With calm, deliberate movements, Westin lifted the bottle and drank, the working muscles of his throat making her mouth dry. The implied threat in his actions was not lost on her.

Then he set the empty container on the edge of her desk and came toward her, buttoning his coat before clasping her hand. His touch burned, even though his skin was cold and wet with condensation. His gaze was as icy as his grip. He'd regroup and come back, she knew.

And she'd be waiting.

Victoria brushed her fingers across his palm again before releasing him. "See you soon, Max."

Max stepped out of the St. John Hotel and cursed vehemently. Gritting his teeth, he fought off the erection that threatened to embarrass him on the crowded sidewalk.

Victoria St. John was trouble.

He'd known that the moment the Council had summoned him. Taming ferals was a task for lesser, newer warlocks. The request had startled him at first, and then intrigued him. When he'd met his prey, however, he understood.

Sly and playful, Victoria moved with the natural grace of a cat. Short black hair and tip-tilted green eyes made her a heady temptation. He'd seen her picture a hundred times and felt nothing more than simple appreciation for a beautiful face. In person, however, Victoria was devastating, all sensuality and heat. She was a bit thin for his tastes, more lithe than curvy, but those legs . . . Those impossibly long legs . . . Soon they would be wrapped around his hips while he stroked his cock deep into her. But it wouldn't be easy. She made that clear with her smile.

She knew who and what he was, which meant the rumors of her power were true. She was no ordinary Familiar.

He shook his head. Darius had been a fool. Familiars needed the strong hand of a warlock or they turned feral. Victoria was a prime example. She was already too wild, defying the High Council at every turn.

She'd also defied *him*.

Both intrigued and attracted, Max mentally ran through the information he'd gathered before approaching her. Victoria was one of the most prominent figures of their kind, her shrewd business dealings taking her from franchising a motel to owning one of the largest chains of upscale hotels in the country. Up until the death of her warlock, she'd been an esteemed member of the magical community. Her wildness since Darius's passing solidified the Council's position that it was best if the pairings were made with mental calculation, rather than through affairs of the heart. Occasionally, love grew anyway such as happened to Victoria, but this was far rarer with Council intervention.

Max rounded the corner and stepped into a side alley. Using his powers, he bridged the distance across town to his penthouse apartment in the blink of an eye. There he paced the acid-washed cement floors restlessly, every nerve on edge. He had no doubt Victoria St. John had stolen her own necklace. It would have been impossible for a human to accomplish the theft.

The museum's security was too advanced. Victoria had done it knowing the brazenness of the act would bring another Hunter after her. The Council worked tirelessly to keep the existence of their kind hidden from humans. Her reckless disregard of their laws had to be stopped before they were revealed.

But *why* was she acting this way? That was what he didn't understand. There had to be a reason beyond lacking a warlock. She was too self-possessed, too calculated. Yes, she needed some reining in, but she wasn't out of control. Before he released her, he was determined to find out what her motivation was.

Exhaling harshly, Max looked around his home, a sprawling loft cloaked in silence and protection spells. The soft gray walls and dark armless sofas had been called cold and barren by some of his subs, but he found the decor soothing, absorbing the energy of the place with the ease of breathing. It would have been simpler to tame her here, where all the tools of his trade were available for his use. But even as he thought this, he realized something different would be required in order to succeed where others had failed.

Collaring Victoria would take a unique approach. Her power was augmented in some way, he'd felt the charge she carried with more than a little surprise. It explained how she had managed to avoid capture all these years. He would have to take her, not just sexually, but in every way. She had to be dominated, as all good Familiars were, but he would have to make her *want* it. She would have to willingly submit—body and soul—in order for the collar to appear, since her powers prevented the usual collaring without consent.

As Max thought of all the things he would do to her, magic coursed through his blood in a heated wave. He couldn't deny how the thought of the taming ahead filled him with anticipation. Not of the task, as he was used to in his private hours, but for the woman upon whom he would work. Just the thought of Victoria's total submission made every muscle in his body harden. All that fire he saw in her eyes, and her careless disregard of how powerful he was—not from ignorance, but for the thrill of the game. For the first time, there was a remote possibility of failure and that whetted his appetite like nothing else ever had.

Max wondered who she'd be assigned to once he finished with her. She would always be stronger than other Familiars, and he refused to break her. A broken Familiar lacked the vitality necessary to be truly helpful.

The hair on his nape prickled with awareness, warning him of the summons before They spoke.

Have you met with the feral? the Council asked. Hundreds of voices speaking in unison.

"She's not feral," he corrected. "Not yet."

She cannot be tamed. Many have tried. Many have failed.

He stilled, wary. "You asked me to capture her. That is what I agreed to. I won't kill her without trying first. If it's an assassination you want, you'll have to find someone else."

There is no other Hunter with your power, They complained. *You know this.*

"So allow me to make an attempt to save her. She's unique. It would be a waste to lose her." Running a hand through his hair, Max blew out his breath. "I will do what is necessary if it comes to that."

We accept your suggestion.

He should have felt reassured by that. But he didn't. "Have you decided where I'm to take her once she's been tamed?"

Of course.

His jaw clenched at the vague answer, the flare of possessiveness unwanted, but there nevertheless. The Dom/sub relationship was unique to each pairing and required a depth of trust not easily passed to another individual. This would be the first time he attempted it, and he wasn't certain he was comfortable with the idea. "Go, then. Leave me to plan."

As the evanescent presence of the Council faded away, the urge to summon Victoria with his power and begin the taming immediately was strong. But he tempered it. His eagerness was ill-placed and inconvenient. He loved hunting, relished the taming, but was not prone to hurrying matters. A proper domination took time, something the visit from the Council told him he didn't have. He had several weeks, at most.

Max growled as his cock hardened in anticipation. Weeks with Victoria.

He was ready to get started.

Two

$\mathcal{R}$estless and edgy, Victoria twirled the sapphire and diamond necklace she'd stolen from the museum around her finger, and wondered if she had finally pushed the High Council too far. A little research into Max Westin had revealed that his usual prey was not their kind, but the Others, those who had crossed over into black magic and could not be saved. He was credited with saving thousands by destroying the few who would wreak havoc with their evil.

The knowledge filled her with concern. Was she now an Other? Considering that Max was rarely sent after anything the Council didn't want dead, it would seem she was. He was a legend, a hero, and on the verge of promotion to the Council. She would have known this had she been an active member of their community instead of an outcast. Which left her with a question she'd spent years trying to answer—was her end goal to die? Did she in truth have a death wish now that Darius was gone? She was strong enough to fight off the collar, but she wasn't strong enough to fight off a warlock of Max's considerable power. And yet she had deliberately goaded his pursuit.

Troubled by the direction of her thoughts, she did what she always did—turned her focus to action, rather than reaction. Since she could not go toe-to-toe with Max and win, she would have to get to him another way.

She would have to seduce him, make him care for her. It was fitting that doing so would be a cruel blow to the Council. It would, in fact, be the ultimate revenge. The Council so rarely promoted anyone. In fact, the last to be so honored had been Darius, and he had refused Them because it would have meant losing her. Rejecting the safety of distant command, he had remained a foot soldier and They had punished him with the most brutal assignments. Leading to his death. The Council would regret that, she would ensure it.

She couldn't wait to get started.

Damn Max Westin for being so stubborn! If he'd come to dinner like she wanted, she could be rubbing against that beautiful male body now. She could be licking his skin, nipping his flesh, fucking his brains out.

Avenging her beloved Darius the only way she knew how.

Max was the perfect Hunter with which to goad the Council. Victoria could picture him easily, tied to her bed and prone for her pleasure. All that rippling muscle and voluptuous power. The Council's golden warlock snared by his own trap.

She blew out her breath, the sudden pang of guilt too disturbing to contemplate. Standing, Victoria loosened the buttons of her sleeveless satin pajama top. She prepared to alter to her feline form when the sound of the doorbell stopped her. Padding leisurely across the golden hardwood floor, she sniffed the air.

Max.

Unexpected pleasure warmed her blood.

Opening the door, she was rendered speechless for a moment. In Armani, Max Westin had been devastating. Now, dressed in low-slung jeans and a fitted t-shirt, his feet bared in leather sandals, he was . . . He was . . .

She purred, the soft vibration filling the air between them with lush promise.

Sneaky bastard. He knew her natural instinct at the sight of his bare feet would be to alter form and rub against them, circling his legs in a blatant display of her willingness. Fighting her very nature, Victoria lifted her arm and leaned against the door jam. Her shirt spread with the pose, revealing her tummy and the under curve of her breast. He shot a brief assessing glance at her display, and then brushed her aside, entering her home like he had every right to do so.

As he crossed to the kitchen with a paper grocery bag in his arms, the candles she had spread around the room flared to life in his wake. The stereo came on, releasing a cacophony of garbled reception before coming to a halt on a classical station. The rich sounds of stringed instruments flooded the room, swelling upward through the exposed ductwork ceiling of her contemporary apartment, setting the stage for what she knew would be a memorable night.

She followed him to the kitchen, where he set the bag on the counter and began to withdraw its contents. Behind him, a pan was magically freed from the overhanging pot rack and settled on the stove.

"The warlock reveals himself," she said softly.

Max smiled. "I am exactly who I said I was."

"An insurance fraud investigator. I checked you out."

"I've recovered on every case."

"So I learned," she said drily. "You're determined to save the world from evildoers, both magical and otherwise."

"Is that such a bad thing?" he challenged softly. "Once, you did the same."

He pulled out a pint of organic cream, and she licked her lips. Perceptive, as all Hunters were, he beckoned a bowl from the cupboard with a flick of his wrist and poured her a ration. Victoria freed the last button on her shirt. A moment later, it and her drawstring pants were pooled on the marble kitchen floor. She waited a second longer, giving him a quick glimpse of what he'd get his fill of later, and then altered shape. With a fluid spring of her feline legs, she made the high leap to the butcher-block counter and crouched over the bowl.

Max ran his hand over her soft black fur. "You're beautiful, kitten," he rumbled in his delicious voice.

She purred in reply.

As she lapped up the cream, Victoria curled her tail around his wrist. His large hand dwarfed her, but she felt safe with him, unusual for an uncollared Familiar around a warlock who lacked a guide.

Hunters were the most powerful of magicians and didn't need the augmentation Familiars provided. They kept the magical world clean, tracking down and dealing with any deviants who fought the command of the High Council.

Others like her.

The blunt tips of his fingers found the spots behind her ears and rubbed. She melted into the countertop.

"Let me finish dinner," he murmured. "And then we'll play."

Max turned away to tend the stove, and she fought the urge to go to him. She lay on the countertop, her chin on her paws watching the muscles of his upper back flex as he chopped vegetables and seared fish. Studying him, she noted the ebony hair that shined with vitality and the firm, proud curve of his ass. She sighed.

She missed having a steady man in her life. Lately the loneliness seemed worse than ever, and she blamed the Council for that. They should have waited until a second witch or warlock/Familiar pairing could have joined them against the Triumvirate, but They failed to temper their eagerness. Unwilling to fail in so important a task, Darius had lost his life in order to succeed. And she had lost her soul mate.

With her heart weighing heavily, Victoria jumped to the floor and circled Max's feet, purring and preening to win his attention. He was, astonishingly, too busy taking care of her to have meaningless sex with her. Too busy cooking for her, and soothing her with music and candlelight.

Her weary soul soaked up the attention greedily.

Moving through eternity without a partner was taking its toll. She couldn't date humans, and she was exiled from her community. There was no one to wait for her or worry about her.

Her work was fulfilling and her success a source of deep pride, but often she wished she could curl up on the couch with a man who cared about her. Loved her. Max was not that man, but he was the first of all the warlocks sent after her who took the time to woo her. Part of her appreciated his efforts. The other part of her understood that he had ulterior motives.

So she wooed him right back, rubbing against his powerful calves with soft, tantalizing purrs.

The road to failure began thusly with all her Hunters. She promised them delight with every brush against their legs, her pheromones scenting the air until they were mad to have her. Due to Darius's gift, she was able to alter her scent from one of submission to one of carnal demand, a primitive challenge to a Hunter's need to be dominant. In effect, a waving red cape to a raging bull.

"It's not so bad," Max soothed in a tone that made her spine arch in pleasure. "There is joy in submission."

Piqued that he remained so casually unaffected, Victoria sauntered away, her tail held high and her head lifted proudly.

Submission. She wasn't suited to it. She was far too strong-willed, far too independent to bow to a man's demands. Darius had known this. He had accepted it, and made exceptions for her so they could live in harmony.

Victoria altered form, and sprawled on the couch naked. From his position in the kitchen, Max had only to turn around and he could see her. His self-control disturbed her, as did the quiet air of command and the steely determination in those gray eyes. He was not a man to be led around by his dick.

She sighed, and waited for him to come to her. No man or warlock could long resist a naked, prone, and willing woman.

Leaning heavily into the counter, Max stared down at the

cutting board and exhaled his frustration. At this moment, he wanted nothing more than to show the beautifully bared woman on the couch all the things he could do to her. For her. It took far more restraint than he was used to exerting to prevent tossing the knife into the sink and doing exactly that. A hard, heavy fucking would help her forget, for a while, the sorrow he felt in her.

His eyes closed as he focused on that faint hint of sadness. The bond between Familiar and warlock always began with this tiny thread of awareness. It was early, too early, for the connection to be there, but it was. There was not enough of it yet to discern the cause of her unhappiness, but Max knew it was not a new distress. She'd carried it for some time.

Strangely, it was that deeper knowledge of her that attracted him now. More so than her beauty. Lust goaded by tenderness was a new sensation for him, one he savored slowly, as he would the first taste of a fine wine. Soft and mellow, it heated his blood just as liquor would.

As he continued to cook, he held on to the feel of his kitten, fostering the bond that he would use to bring her in from the fringes and back into the fold.

"Dinner's ready," he called out after a time.

Victoria stared up at the ceiling and wondered how Max could be so indifferent to her brazen offering of sex. Petulant, she said, "I want to eat in here."

"Suit yourself," he answered easily. She heard one of the dining chairs pulled away from the table, and a moment later the clink of silverware against china. Mouth agape, she bolted upright.

"Ummm . . ." Max's deep hum of enjoyment made goose

bumps race across her skin. Then the rich scent of seared ahi and cream hit her nostrils and made her tummy growl.

She stood, and stomped into the kitchen, where she found only one setting—the one Max was seated in front of. Hands on her hips, her feline sensibilities offended, she snapped, "What about me?"

"Do you intend to join me now?"

"I planned to."

Pushing away from the table, he rose to his full height, dwarfing her, a difference made more noticeable by her own state of undress. He offered her his chair, his apparent indifference to her bare body making her fists clench. Victoria plopped into the seat with an audible exhalation. This was not at all how she'd planned to corrupt him.

He reached for the long-tined fork. Spearing a piece of the nearly raw fish, Max dipped it in cream, and brought it to her lips. Startled, she stared up at him.

"Open."

Before she realized it was a command, her lips parted and accepted the offering. Designed for her palate, the tastes blended together to form a delight for her senses. Max stood beside her, one hand on the back of her chair, caging her in while he prepared another bite. Her eyes met his in silent query.

"It's a warlock's duty to care for his pet."

"I'm not your pet." *But it felt wonderful in any case.*

"For now, you are."

She hated to admit it, but his unwavering confidence aroused her. Her small breasts grew heavy, tender, the nipples peaked hard for his touch. Obligingly, his hand left the chair back and cupped the soft swell. Victoria gasped at the unexpected intimacy, and Max slipped the next bite into her mouth. As she chewed slowly, savoring the singular meal, his skilled fingertips toyed with her nipple.

"To submit is not to be weak," he crooned in a husky, hypnotic tone. "You would not be less of a woman, kitten, but so much more of one."

She shook her head fiercely even as she squeezed her thighs together, fighting the aching depth of lust she did not want to feel. The soft rolling and tugging of Max's fingers on her nipple made her blood hot. As his arousal rose to meet hers, his skin warmed and filled the air with the faint scent of his cologne. The prominent bulge of his hard-on was eye level, and she couldn't help but stare. The danger inherent in wanting him and his implacable arrogance turned her on to such an extent that she was panting in her chair. Her back arched helplessly, begging for more.

"It's in your nature," he murmured, his mouth to her ear. "The desire to be taken. To have the choice ripped from you so all you have to do is feel. Imagine my hands and mouth on your breasts . . . my fingers, tongue, and cock thrusting between your legs. . . . Your only task would be to enjoy the pleasure I can give you. Imagine the freedom in that."

Freedom. Submission. The words could not be used together. They were mutually exclusive, but every time Victoria opened her mouth to retort, he filled it with food.

He continued to feed and fondle her until she writhed in the seat. Her skin was hot and tight, her cleft wet and creamy. Max knew all about her. He would have studied Familiars with precision and her in particular. It was his mission to hunt those who defied the Council. He knew Familiars craved to be touched and well fed. His approach was unusual, and therefore caught her off guard. They usually tried to fuck her into submission, not coddle her into it.

Soon her belly was full, which normally made her sleepy. But not tonight. The burning lust in her veins kept her from napping. But still she was languid. Pliable. Max lifted and carried her to her room, and she was unable to protest. She wanted to feel him inside her like she wanted to breathe. Still, she wasn't a fool. With a softly spoken word, Victoria bound his powers.

His smile told her he felt what she'd done. It wasn't just any smile, but one that promised she'd pay.

It only made her hotter.

Max set her on her feet, and turned her to face away from him. Anticipation rippled down her spine, making her shiver and breathe shallowly. With a firm, irrefutable hold on the scruff of her neck, he pressed her forward until she bent at the waist, face down in her bed.

"Max?"

As he pulled away, his teeth scraped her shoulder with seductive portent and before she could blink, her hands were bound behind her.

"What the hell?" Her heart raced in near panic. She couldn't believe he would move so quickly. She had never been bound. The sudden feeling of helplessness reminded her of the way she'd felt when Darius stood in the midst of deadly swirls of magic and she could only watch, useless. "No!" Victoria struggled wildly.

"Hush, kitten." His large body came over hers, a warm physical blanket. With his hands on either side of her head, he nuzzled his cheek against hers, his voice far huskier than usual. "I won't hurt you. Not ever."

"I—You—"

"You can't bind my powers," he murmured. "You're strong, but not that strong."

"I don't like this, Max." Her voice was a plaintive whisper.

Then one of his hands lifted from the mattress. She felt it working against the curve of her ass just before she heard the slow rasp of his zipper lowering. To her amazement, the arousal that had died flared to life again.

"You're so tense." He licked a slow, wet trail along the length of her spine. "All you have to do is lie there and come."

Suddenly, she couldn't see, her vision blocked by some spell he'd cast. Victoria went completely still, her breath caught in her throat. She'd never felt so completely at the mercy of someone else.

Between her legs she ached with an arousal that made her writhe. Despite what her mind said, her instinctual nature could not be denied.

"Look how ready you are." His fingers stroked between her legs, gliding through the creamy evidence of how excited she was. "It must be exhausting fighting against yourself all the time."

"Fuck you," she spat. Though his tone was matter-of-fact and not smug, she still felt suppressed. Restrained.

Dominated.

"Actually, I'm going to fuck *you*. And you're going to trust me enough to enjoy it."

"I can't trust you. I don't know you. I only know what you want, which is the exact opposite of what I want."

"Is it?" he asked patiently. "You'll know me by the time I'm done. We'll start with sex and work our way out."

Victoria snorted. "How original."

He paused, and she knew she'd scored a direct hit. She thought that would be the end of it.

Then against the back of her legs she felt the roughness of his jeans. "Aren't you going to undress?" she breathed, her already keen senses now painfully acute from her blindness.

"No."

One word. No explanation. She struggled, but was stilled by the warm, broad head of his cock stroking against her clit.

"Spread your legs wider, Victoria."

She didn't move. Damned if she'd help him tame her, arrogant bastard.

He sank in, forcing her slick tissues to spread for him, to accept him. Just an inch. Then he withdrew. Rubbing the now creamy tip against her, Max teased her, and then pressed inside her again. Just that one inch. She buried her head in the comforter and groaned, her sex spasming, trying to pull him in to where she needed him.

"If you spread your legs, you can have what you want."

Victoria lifted her head. "I want *you* tied to the bed so I can torture you. Not the other way around."

His rumbling laughter made her shiver. The fact was, no matter what Max did or said, he attracted her. "But you wouldn't be enjoying that nearly as much as this."

"Screw the games, Max. Can't we just fuck?"

"I want to fuck you like this, angled just the way I want you."

"What about what I want?" she complained.

"You want the same thing, kitten. You just wish you didn't.

You're so tight like this, your cunt is like a velvet fist. I'll have to work my way into you . . ."

Max waited with the same studious patience he'd displayed since meeting her, all the while the head of his cock stroked into the mouth of her pussy in silent enticement. Her traitorous body beckoned him with a soft ripple. She was soaked and hot, more than ready.

She briefly considered altering and walking away, but then she wouldn't have sex with Max and that just wouldn't do. So, with her pride smarting, Victoria widened her stance. He'd pay later.

Immediately he surged inside, going deep and then deeper still until she couldn't breathe, couldn't think, every part of her focused on the thick pulsing cock that filled her too full.

Gasping, her back arched as his short nails scraped lightly across her hips. He leaned over her. Dominated her. As his rippling stomach touched her bound hands she felt the dampness of his sweat through his t-shirt.

The warlock was not as controlled as he appeared.

Taking what little power she could, she clutched his shirt in her hands, holding him to her.

Hands on the mattress to support his weight, Max began to shaft her in long, deep drives. The angle of his penetration stroked with tantalizing pressure inside her, and he varied his thrusts, rubbing high and then low in an expert inner massage.

It was slow and far too easy, his hips pumping in timed, measured rhythm. Unable to see, she pictured how it must look, Max fully clothed, his ass clenching and releasing as he fucked her bound body. She quivered and began to purr. He growled in response, the vibration traveling the length of his body and into his thrusting cock.

"Do you feel weak?" he asked, his voice guttural and taunting. "Do you feel reduced because your body serves my pleasure and not your own?"

She wanted to retort, to argue, to fight, but she couldn't. It felt too good doing nothing but taking what he gave her. She was a cat after all and inherently lazy.

"Inherently submissive," he corrected. He moved one hand to cup her thigh and pulled it wider so he could fuck deeper. Now every plunge of his cock brought his tight, heavy balls against her clit.

He'd read her thoughts, she thought with what part of her brain was still functional.

The taming had begun.

With a soft hiss, she tightened around him. He cursed softly and shuddered, his body betraying him.

Suddenly, she grasped that he was as helpless as she. She'd attempted to use her body to entice him, and he'd succumbed. Despite the outward control he displayed, Max had started the evening with an entirely different approach and had dissolved from that into lust that could not be denied. Even now, his fingers bruised her hips, his thighs strained against hers, his labored breathing sounded loudly in the room.

Realizing that she was not alone in this unexpected physical fascination, she relaxed, sinking into the bed with a moan. It was not surrender. It was a stalemate.

Victoria's mouth curved in a catlike smile.

Three

Max lifted the cup of coffee to his lips and stared out the window at the St. John Hotel directly across the street. He took deep, even breaths, his thoughts fully focused on clearing his mind. Excitement and anticipation coursed through his veins, and he studiously worked to temper them.

Control. Where was his? It was undeniable that when he was with Victoria hunger drove him, not his mission.

His kitten was a tigress in bed, one who rolled, scratched, and bit with abandoned fervor. Tying her to the brass headboard had been a necessary delight. One he'd repeated often over the last two weeks.

I don't like this, Max, she'd said every time. But with her nipples hard against his tongue, he'd known the truth. She quaked, cursed, writhed, and the sight always made him so hard he'd have to grit his teeth to hold back his lust. Then he'd give up and fuck her for hours, long past exhaustion, abandoning his assignment in favor of overwhelming pleasure.

And the Council knew it.

Your lack of progress displeases us, They'd complained just an hour ago.

"You've given me very little time," he'd retorted.

We think no amount of time will be sufficient for taming the feral. She is beyond rehabilitation.

"She is not." He'd exhaled sharply. "You've never rushed me like this before, and she's the toughest case I've ever been given."

Decades have passed. Our patience is thin.

Turning away from both the window and the memory with a low curse, Max caught up his coat and left the café. Time had just run out. He couldn't fail in this. Failure would cost him more than loss of pride. It would cost Victoria her life.

He crossed the busy thoroughfare and entered the St. John by way of the revolving glass doors, waiting until he was mid-rotation before using his power to move up to the top floor, where Victoria was hard at work. The thought of her occupied at her desk made his dick ache. He adored intelligent women, and Victoria was more cunning than most. She was also tough as nails.

The only time she'd been truly vulnerable was on the brink of orgasm, so he'd kept her there, time and time again, absorbing the sudden flood of her thoughts and recollections. Feeling the love she'd once had for Darius and the aching sadness of loss. Those glimpses of her soul always moved him to orgasm, the feeling of connection so profound it stole his breath.

He grit his teeth as his cock swelled further. He'd come

more since meeting her than he would have thought possible. It was why he had made so little headway. A proper taming required restraint on the part of the Hunter. He should have been finding his release elsewhere, tempering his desire, but no other woman appealed.

"Good afternoon, Mr. Westin," the receptionist greeted with a come-hither smile.

With a snap of his fingers, she had no recollection of his visit, her memory wiped clean in the blink of an eye. All she knew was that her boss was too busy to be disturbed, and she would take messages and deny visitors until she was told otherwise.

Max entered Victoria's lair without knocking, setting in place a simple glamour that prevented any passerby from seeing their coming activities through the glass office wall.

She looked up, arched a brow, and set her pen down. "Max."

His name. One word. In that soft purr, it was an aphrodisiac and he was not immune as he should be.

"Hello, kitten." He smiled at the soft shiver he felt from her. She was not immune either.

"I'm busy."

"You're about to be," he agreed, setting aside his coffee and summoning a beautifully wrapped box on her desk.

Her mouth curved in a sensual smile that made his blood heat. "A gift? How delightful."

Long, elegant fingers plucked at the lavender iridescent ribbon and tore at the royal blue wrapping. Inside rested an ornate wooden box. He watched as her fingertips drifted over the phrase that was carved there: *Only within my bonds will you truly know freedom.*

Victoria said nothing, but he watched her with a Hunter's perception and noted the sudden appearance of erect nipples beneath her white silk blouse. Her hand lifted to engage his vision, holding aloft a set of velvet-lined nipple clamps connected by a delicate gold chain.

"I was wondering when you were planning to get around to the toys," she said, a tad breathlessly. "You've waited longer than most."

The intimation that he was nothing special, merely another in a long string of annoyances, forced his hand. Furiously swirling air filled the room, scattering the papers on the desk and thrusting Victoria backward. Max stalked toward her, his gaze narrowed, his open palm closing swiftly into a fist, bringing her to an abrupt stop just a scant inch away from the window.

Her green eyes were wide, her lips parted on panting breaths, her chest rising and falling in apparent fear. He, however, knew it to be intense arousal. He could feel her in his thoughts, their bond building with every moment spent together. The surge of power inside her, a careful blending of magic and Familiar enhancement, made him groan aloud with his own overpowering lust. Never in his life had he felt this way about a woman. It felt almost as if he'd found the perfect fit to a puzzle piece. His fingertips itched with the magic coursing through him—magic strengthened by his proximity to Victoria.

"Kitten," he growled, reaching her. He thrust his hands into her cropped hair and pressed her back against the glass, her feet suspended a few feet above the ground. Eye-level with him.

She purred and nuzzled against him, her silver hoop earrings cold against his cheek, and then too hot. He stepped back, his power pinning her to the scenic view of the city behind her. Her arms were held motionless beside her head, her breasts thrusting wantonly toward him in the submissive pose. Only here, in the seat of her corporate influence, would a true taming be possible. She was ruler here. Until he arrived.

That was the lesson to be learned.

As he reached for the buttons of his shirt and freed them, magic mimicked his movements with Victoria's blouse. He smiled as he felt his belt loosen, pleased with her initiative in exerting her own power to undress him.

"A nooner?" she murmured, before licking her lips.

"An all-afternooner," he corrected, shrugging out of his shirt.

"You're insatiable."

"You love it."

Max watched with heated anticipation as the bra clasp between her breasts snapped open and then separated. The nipple clamps rose up from the floor and then clipped into place, her reaction to the sudden pressure a low hiss from between clenched teeth. The sight of those pale, firm breasts capped with swollen, reddened nipples and the slender chain made freeing his cock from its confinement necessary.

"Oooh, Max," she purred, moving sinuously against the window as he dropped his pants. "What a big cock you have."

He gave her his best wolfish grin, enjoying her playfulness in the face of her helplessness. "The better to screw you with, my dear."

The side zipper of her thin skirt lowered and then the garment fell to the carpeted floor along with her black lace thong and stiletto heels. "After," he summoned the remaining contents of the box into his open palm, "I screw you with this."

Victoria swallowed hard at the sight of the slightly curved dildo in his hand. It was long and thick, close in size, shape, and coloring to Max's cock. He lubed it generously, his gaze never leaving hers.

She pouted. "I don't want that thing. I want you."

Max faltered a moment at her words, then moved quickly, taking her mouth with deep-seated hunger, distracting her from the tightening bond between them.

I want you. Such simple words, but for her, the words imperiled. It wasn't quite the "needing" required to make the collar appear, but it was close enough to cause a quickening inside him. He shouldn't feel anything more than triumph at her words, but he did. Much more.

It was what he'd hoped for, the result he had set out to achieve, but he hadn't expected it to happen so fast. He had been certain he'd have to drive her mad first. He couldn't do it while he was inside her, like he had done with every other Familiar he'd tamed. When he was joined to Victoria, the Council faded from his perception, leaving just the two of them lost in each other. The only needs he cared about were his own, and the Council could go to hell.

As he breathed deeply of her scent, his eyes squeezed shut, his chest heaving against hers, his fingers slipping between her legs to rub her clit. He felt possessive and needy. God, all morning since he'd left her he'd wanted her. Only hours apart. Too long. Knowing their time together was temporary, he coveted every moment and hated to share her with work or anyone else.

Irreverent, saucy, mischievous—she was a cat through and

through. She both soothed and incited him, a dichotomy that left him satisfied on every front.

And he was preparing her for an eternity with another man.

The knowledge made his jaw ache, and his chest tighten painfully. He shoved the thought away, and concentrated on the here and now. At least she'd be alive. If he had to lose her, better to another warlock than to death.

Whimpering into his mouth as he stroked her slick cunt, Victoria tried to writhe, but couldn't fight the force that held her. "Max," she breathed into his mouth. "Let me touch you."

He shook his head, unwilling to break away from the kiss.

"I want to touch you, damn it!" She jerked her mouth away.

"You should want what *I* want." His voice was rough, harsh. "My pleasure is yours. My hunger is yours."

"Is your need mine, too?" Victoria asked softly, her gaze riveted to the large man who stood before her. She heard his teeth grind in response to her query and his touch left her.

There was an urgency to his seduction that had never been there before. To come to her during the day, when they would have been together within hours . . .

She inhaled sharply. How often had she caught herself day-dreaming about him, reliving moments from the long night before? He cooked for her every night, and fed her by hand. He showered with her, and washed her hair. There were rough moments, too, along with the tender. Moments of high passion—like when he'd come through her front door and dragged her to the floor, saying hello with guttural cries and drugging thrusts of his beautiful cock deep inside her. Never asking permission. Taking what he desired as if the use of her body was his right.

The attention had seduced her, reminding her of the intimate connection between warlock and Familiar. But the woman within her had also been captivated. She wielded great power in her human life. She was responsible for the thousands of employees who worked under her command. There was relief and pleasure to be found in turning herself entirely into Max's dominant keeping. Darius had treated her as equal. Max never let her forget that he held the power.

But now his words betrayed him, revealing the depth of his affection for her.

You should want what your Master wants. His pleasure is yours. His hunger is yours. His need is yours.

But Max had inserted himself as her Master. And the need to accept him was nearly overwhelming.

When she was with him, the restlessness that had plagued her for so long was soothed immeasurably. She wasn't alone when she was with Max. Aside from Darius, he was the only man to ever make her feel that way. She'd put on needed weight, finding joy in sharing her meals and life with someone who wanted her to be happy. And she was, because he made sure of it. Yes, the single most important aspect of their relationship was satisfying him, but what satisfied Max was pleasuring her.

Victoria watched him warily as he approached. The dildo, glistening with lube, was aimed straight at the juncture between her legs. Max leaned forward and licked across her lips. "Open up, kitten."

Mutinously, she defied him. "Make me."

With a slight flick of his hand, magic forced her legs apart.

She creamed, softening further, some traitorous part of her heritage relishing the taming, knowing she was about to be pleasured beyond bearing, and she didn't have to do a damned thing.

"Look how wet you are," he praised, rubbing the smooth tip up and down her drenched slit. He pressed his mouth against her ear and whispered, "You love a hard cock in you."

"I love *your* hard cock in me." She gasped, her pussy clenching tight in an effort to capture the thick head that teased her opening.

"Let's play first," he rumbled, sliding the dildo a scant inch inside her. She tried to grind her hips down onto it, but couldn't.

"Max!"

"Shush, I'll give it to you." With deft twists of his wrist, he pumped it softly, working it inside her, his other hand catching the chain between her breasts and tugging gently. A deep ache built within her breasts, spreading through her torso, making her cry out.

"Easy," he crooned, thrusting gently, finally spearing home with breathtaking expertise.

Her eyes met his, trying to understand why he took her like this, what it was he wanted from her so she could give it to him. Then she gave up, her eyes drifting closed, her body shuddering with pleasure as he fucked her with long, smooth strokes.

"Please," she whispered, her hot cheek pressed to the cool glass.

"Please what?" His tongue swiped across the pinched tip

of a tormented nipple, then his mouth closed around both it and the clamp, sucking in rhythm to the rutting between her thighs.

"I want you."

Max released her breast, and quickened his pace. Her hips rocked as much as they were able, her cries desperate, her clit swollen and throbbing for the slight touch that would send her into orgasm. Deep inside, the feel of the wide, flared head stroking along the walls of her pussy made her head thrash from side to side, the only part of her body she was allowed to move.

He groaned and leaned against her, his skin coated in a fine sheen of sweat. His tongue licked the shell of her ear and then thrust inside.

"Don't you want me, Max?" she gasped, dying from the need to climax, to move, to have more than a fake cock could ever give her.

"You drive me insane." He nuzzled his damp forehead against her cheek.

"Is that a 'yes'?"

If it was . . . if he felt the connection she did . . . What she wouldn't give to find love a second time. Perhaps, in the end, it wouldn't be with Max, but this was the closest she'd come to that emotion in over two centuries.

Suddenly his hand was at her throat, his mouth over hers, his knees braced against the window to support the thrusts of his hand.

Give me what I want.

The melding of his thoughts with hers was all the impetus she needed. Part of the taming was his ability to read her thoughts, but for her to know his meant the connection ran both ways.

The tension fled her body. Her sex spasmed with want, clutching greedily for what it *needed* ...

"Please," she breathed, aching to hold him. "I need you."

Max tilted Victoria's head back a split second before the collar appeared. The thin black ribbon looked so innocuous, but it bound her more than chains ever could. It would fade when she was paired with a warlock, become a part of her, just as her new master would.

The sight of the collar and the submission it signified made cum dribble from the head of Max's aching cock, every cell in his body flaring with masculine triumph. He yanked the dildo free and tossed it away, releasing her from his spell, catching her limp, willing body in a protective embrace.

He'd almost given in, he had wanted her so badly. Feeling her body grasping for him, hungry for him, had driven him crazy. The only thing that held him back was concern for her. If he failed to bring her back from the edge, They would kill her. And that would kill him.

Clutching her close, Max used his powers to take them home—his home. There he lowered her gently to his velvet-covered bed and then cupped her thigh, spreading her wide. The sight of the glistening lips of her sex and tiny pussy made his balls draw up. The look in her eyes made his heart ache.

Hours. That's all they had left.

He climbed over her, admiring the new curves she'd acquired with careful tending. Under his care, she'd lost the signs of neglect. As he caught one of her wrists and pulled it over her head, he never took his eyes from her, using magic to pull the velvet rope from the bedpost and bind her.

"Max." A whisper, no more than that, as she lifted her other arm without urging and used her own power to restrain herself.

Victoria was the most powerful woman he'd ever known, both in their world and the world they shared with humans. Her submission of that power to his demands was a gift of such magnitude it captured his heart. His eyes burned, his throat clenched tight.

His kitten. *His.*

He took her then, in a swift sure thrust that joined them so tightly there was no separation. A raw sound tore from his throat as she climaxed instantly, sucking his cock with ripples of pleasure, luring him to come in her with hard, fierce spurts. Holding her shivering body tightly to his, Max pumped gently, draining his seed while prolonging her pleasure, absorbing her cries with pure infatuation.

Later, he laced his fingers with hers and rode her bound body again. Harder this time, releasing his passion in a brutal taking, his hips battering hers, his cock plunging deep.

Victoria accepted his lust with such beauty, her voice hoarse, her words barely audible over his labored breathing.

"*Yes ... yes ... yes ...*"

Taking all that he was, blossoming like a flower beneath him, lush with such promise. The places he could take her, the things he could teach her, the freedom he could give her ...

But he was a Hunter groomed to join the Council, and They didn't keep Familiars.

So Max took what he could, his tongue and lips working at her breast, drawing on her with hungry pulls, worrying the hard nipple against the roof of his mouth. His hands pinned her down, kept her still for the steady rise and fall of his hips, his cock working her into endless pleasure, giving her no rest, afraid to stop touching her. Afraid to lose her.

Keep her.

The compulsion rose up so unexpectedly that his rhythm faltered, suspending him at the deepest point of a downward plunge, his cock scalded by the hot clasp of her cunt.

"No!" she cried, struggling beneath him. "Don't stop. Please . . ."

How could he walk away? She'd sacrificed the life she'd built for herself to reenter his.

He would do the same for her. He *needed* to do the same for her.

"Never." He growled and crushed her to him, resuming his claiming, his flushed cheek pressed to hers. "I'll never stop. You're mine. *Mine.*"

Victoria summoned the black robe Familiars wore when facing the Council and dressed silently. She'd preserved the garment all these years, saving it for the day she would face Them and exact her revenge. Now she donned it with a different purpose in mind.

As she prepared to leave, her eyes never strayed from the sleeping form on the bed. Max's powerful body sprawled facedown, the red satin sheets riding low on his hips. Gorgeous.

She ached to touch him, to wake him, to look into those molten silver eyes one last time.

How dangerous he was, even in slumber.

Tears fell unchecked.

Lost in her, his mind had lowered its guards, his thoughts and feelings pouring into her in a flood of longing and affection that destroyed. He was willing to give up all that he'd worked for to keep her, and she couldn't let him do it.

She couldn't lose him like she lost Darius. The Council would be furious at being thwarted a second time. Their spite had cost her one love. She refused to let it cost her another.

Better to lose him to a life apart from her than to death.

So she covered her mouth to muffle her pain, and left him.

Four

The moment Max woke from the depths of sheer physical exhaustion, he knew she was gone. Their connection was such that he had felt Victoria inside him ever since the collar had appeared. Now the warmth she gave him was no longer there, leaving him cold.

But he wasn't alone.

Once again, you exceeded our expectations, the Council said, in a tone laced with satisfaction. *The Familiar is returned to the fold, a result she says would not have been possible without your power and expertise. We are pleased.*

Rolling out of bed, Max tugged on a pair of loose-fitting trousers, his heart racing in near panic. "Where is she?"

She is preparing for the joining ceremony.

"*What?*" He paused and glanced at the clock by his bed, his fists clenching. Two hours ago he'd been balls deep inside her. Now she was bonding forever to another man? "What's the goddamned rush? I just collared her! The training wasn't finished."

How could she?

Black rage rolled over him.

We felt it would be safest, and most effective, to partner her quickly. Her warlock will train her to suit him.

"Who is he?"

Gabriel was selected. He was the only warlock strong enough, aside from you.

Max's jaw ached from gritting his teeth. Gabriel was powerful, considered handsome, as popular with women as Max was, but the other warlock stayed far away from the darker edge of magic. To Max it was a weakness. Gabriel had a line he wouldn't cross and it opened him to failure. Weakness like that would give Victoria too much leeway. She needed an iron fist. Craved it. Max had only one vulnerability, and it was one he needed to control her.

Victoria herself.

There was no line he wouldn't cross to achieve his aims.

And he proved it by abandoning his home, his ambitions, and the life he knew to go after her.

Victoria stared at her reflection as the handmaidens adjusted her robes for the ceremony ahead. Her eyes were red-rimmed, bloodshot, bruised from lack of sleep and too much crying.

She'd forgotten who Max was, seeing him only through smitten eyes, failing to remember that he was a Hunter and next in line to ascend to the Council. He'd spent centuries working toward his goal, and two weeks working on her—one of many assignments in his past, with more to come in his future. He would forget her in time.

The thought made her heart hurt, the pain so piercing she panted with it.

Waving her attendants away, Victoria caught the edge of the vanity and gulped down desperate breaths. She'd been out of the loop so long, she had no idea who Gabriel was, but the handmaidens raved about her luck. Yes, she would pine for the man who'd taken over her body and filled it with mind-numbing pleasure, but perhaps, in a decade or two, she could come to tolerate Gabriel's touch . . .

"You'll never know, kitten," rumbled a deep, familiar voice behind her.

Her gaze lifted and met stormy gray.

"Max," she breathed, her palms growing damp at the sight of him. Bare-chested, barefooted, wearing only trousers that hung low around his lean hips. His shoulders so broad, his golden skin stretched over beautifully defined muscles. A predator.

Her mouth dried, her breasts swelled with desire, as if he hadn't just fucked her into exhaustion mere hours ago.

He came toward her with his sultry, long-legged stride. She was held motionless by his stare, forgetting to breathe until her lungs burned, then she gasped and cried out as his hand cupped the back of her head. His strong fingers pinched strands of her hair and tugged roughly, bending her to his will. She stared up at him in a haze of fear and desire, the flush of anger on his face enough to frighten her. And arouse her.

"I'm keeping you," he rasped, just before he took her parted lips with possessive hunger.

Having thought him lost to her, she melted in his arms. He anchored her, even as he brought her to heel. His breathing labored, he turned his head, his cheek rubbing against hers, absorbing her tears.

"The Council will punish you," she cried, her voice breaking. "I—I can't bear to lose you."

"But you were about to." He licked deep into her mouth, making her moan and open to him, silently begging for more. He obliged her, groaning, his tongue stroking along hers with so much skill it left her breathless. One arm supported her back, the other hand cupped her breast and kneaded it with the aggressive pressure she'd come to relish and crave.

"Let me be the instrument of your revenge," he whispered darkly, his lips moving against hers.

A gift. For her.

Victoria swallowed hard, stunned by his statement and the ramifications of it. "Max."

He held her gaze. "You have your business interests to occupy your daylight hours, but your private hours are mine. You will serve, obey, and please me. You will never question an order or deny me anything. I'll do things to your body that will test your limits. Sometimes, you'll want to tell me 'no,' but you'll do what I want regardless. That is your commitment to me."

He hugged her tightly to him, burying his face in the tender space between her neck and shoulder. His voice lowered and came gruffly: "My commitment is to care for you, and provide for you in every way. If you need your revenge to be free of the past, I will deliver the means to you. You are my greatest treasure, Victoria. I will always value and treat you as such."

Her arms came around him, her lashes wet and vision blurry. "I want the Triumvirate."

To give her this, he would have to skirt the very Council

he'd aspired to for so long. There was more to that long-ago night than she knew, and the danger was mortal.

Max nodded his understanding and agreement without hesitation, but the tic in his jaw betrayed him. "Will you love me like you loved him? Can you?"

She released a deep breath in an audible rush. Her heart reached out to him, revealing the many facets of her affection and adoration, the feelings she had for Max so different from what she'd felt for Darius, but just as powerful, and growing every day. She was beginning to see how much of herself she'd kept away from Darius, and how much of herself she'd already shared with Max—the man who'd shown her how to embrace her nature and revel in it. Safe in his embrace.

"Yes, Max," she promised. "So much."

His power swelled in response to her passion, flowing into her, and she enhanced it. The soul-deep thrumming that coursed through them was almost overwhelming. They would have to train, relearn everything they knew, find a way to control it. Together.

I can't wait to get started. Max's confident voice in her mind gave her courage.

The task ahead wouldn't be easy . . .

You don't like things easy, kitten.

Victoria offered her mouth to him and he took it, his chest rumbling with laughter as her lips curved against his in a cat-like smile.

That Old Black Magic

One

There was an indefinable something about the tall, darkly clad man traversing the sidewalk. That mysterious quality compelled lingering glances from every window-seat reveler in Richie's Diner. He appeared not to notice, his gaze direct and unwavering, his purpose set and immutable.

It was hard to pinpoint what it was that arrested attention. Was it the impressive breadth of his shoulders and the way his inky black locks hung past them like a mane? Was it the way he moved with sensual purpose, every stride elegant yet predatory? Or was it his face, classically yet brutally gorgeous, all hard planes and angles, rigid jaw combined with beautifully etched lips?

Perhaps it was simply that it was Christmas Eve, a time

when he should be home, warm and safe with the ones he loved. Not out in the snow, alone and unsmiling.

He had eyes of gray, like a brewing storm, and an air of complete confidence that clearly stated he was not a man to be crossed without penalty.

"That man could fuck a gal to a screaming orgasm. Guaranteed," Richie's wife said breathlessly to her cousin.

"Where do I sign up?"

The diner was closed to customers, yet filled to capacity with Richard Bowes's family and friends. Children manned the soft-serve machine, making shakes, while the men cooked and told bawdy jokes in the kitchen. Frank Sinatra sang holiday songs through the speakers, and laughter filled the air with the joy of the season.

Pausing at the corner, the hunk outside held out both arms, and a lithe black cat that had not been visible from the window booths jumped agilely into his embrace. It had been snowing hard earlier and featherlight flakes still drifted in the random gusts, yet the animal's luxurious ebony coat was unmarred by the weather. The man, too, did not appear to be wet or cold.

He held the feline with reverence, his fingers rubbing behind its ears and stroking down its arching spine. It climbed his chest and looked over his shoulder, emerald green eyes staring back at the diner occupants. Nuzzling the top of its head against his cheek, the cat seemed to smile smugly at the coveting gazes from women in the diner.

There wasn't a single Bowes female who didn't wish to be that cat.

For a long moment, the flashing Christmas lights in the windows cast rainbow hues on glossy fur and rich locks, creating a unique yet beautiful holiday scene. Then the man continued on.

He crossed the street and rounded a corner, disappearing.

Max Westin growled softly at the feel of a rough feline tongue stroking rhythmically across the sensitive skin behind his ear.

"Kitten . . . ," he warned.

You're delicious, Victoria purred in his mind.

"I can see why upper-level warlocks don't keep Familiars." He held her closer to ease the sting of his words. "You're a distraction."

I'm necessary, she retorted, laughing. *You couldn't live without me.*

He didn't reply; they both knew it was true. He loved her with a deep, saturating abandon and relished the bond they shared as warlock and Familiar. She was with him every moment, her thoughts and emotions melding with his, her power augmenting his. Even when physical distance separated them, they were always together. He couldn't breathe without her anymore. She was a part of him, and he wouldn't have it any other way.

Once a Hunter for the Council that ruled over all "magic-kind," he had been assigned only the most difficult of tasks—vanquishing those who had crossed over into black magic and could not be saved. He had been groomed to join the Council, an honor bestowed so rarely that few remembered the last time such a promotion had occurred.

Then, They'd tasked him with one last assignment—collar or kill Victoria St. John, a Familiar driven feral by grief over the loss of her warlock.

Max would never forget his first sighting of her and how powerfully she'd affected him. Slender and long-legged, with green sloe eyes and cropped black hair, she had the inherent sensuality of a cat and the body of a woman built for sex.

A deeply rooted part of him had known she belonged to him from the moment they met. Some part of her had known it, too, yet they'd played a cat-and-mouse game until it could not be played any longer. Until the Council stepped in and forced them to make a choice—the Council's dictates or each other.

Neither of them had hesitated to choose their love, regardless of the penalty.

I feel them, she said, her throaty voice bereft of the teasing playfulness of a moment before.

"Me, too."

The Triumvirate. They were responsible for the death of Victoria's previous warlock, Darius. He, too, had been groomed for the Council, the last warlock so honored before Max had caught Their notice. Angered by Darius's decision to pair with Victoria instead of accepting a Council seat, They had retaliated by sending Darius and Victoria after the Triumvirate alone.

Darius should have refused, knowing his death would be the inevitable outcome of such an uneven match. He should have fought to stay with Victoria, to protect her from the machinations of the Council.

That's what Max would have done.

Yet you hunt them now, she murmured.

"For you."

It was the promise he'd made to her when he claimed her

for his own—her submission in return for his destruction of the Triumvirate. She had not asked it of him until he insisted, but it was a Master's prerogative to ensure that his sub had what they needed to be happy. Victoria needed closure; he would give it to her.

I love you.

He felt the undeniable truth of her feelings deep in his soul. The shining brightness of Victoria's love was so powerful that it kept the darkness inside him in the shadows where it belonged. Skirting the edges of black magic was perilous, because the dark side was seductive. If he didn't have Victoria to anchor him, Max wasn't sure what he would have become over the centuries.

"I love you, too, kitten."

The snowfall picked up again, making it hard to see. The wind grew colder, blowing on the diagonal, pelting flurries at them from the side. They should be home, entangled naked before the fireplace, sweating from carnal exertion. Not shivering from a chill that came as much from the inside as the outside.

Shielding them in magic, Max kept them dry as they turned the street corner and then again into a trash-strewn alley. The sudden blizzard was a show of force from the Triumvirate, a reminder that the three brothers were forbiddingly powerful. It was two against three as it was, but the odds were less favorable than even that. The Triumvirate drew power from the Source of All Evil. Max and Victoria had only each other. When their resources were depleted, they would have no other recourse. The Council would not help them. They'd refused to sanction this battle, knowing it was what Max and

Victoria wanted more than anything. When it came to holding grudges, the Council was in a class by itself.

Is it worth it?

He paused midstep, startled by her thought.

Victoria leaped down from his shoulder to the wet pavement. She altered form instantly, leaving her standing before him naked and endlessly alluring, her only adornment a black ribbon around her neck.

His collar. The sight of it and the knowledge of what it symbolized aroused him with violent alacrity.

"Gods, you're beautiful," he rasped, admiring the ripe, curvy perfection of her lithe body. With a snap of his fingers she was clothed from head to toe in formfitting black Lycra. Her figure was his to enjoy and no other's.

When they met, she'd been too thin, a manifestation of neglect wrought by centuries spent without a Master to care for her. Familiars needed to be fed and groomed, stroked and indulged. They also needed discipline, and she'd had none, not even with Darius, who, despite his extraordinary power and skill, had been too flexible to control a Familiar as willful as Victoria St. John.

"I'm not sure I want to do this, Max," she said, stepping into his arms.

Power pulsed through his veins at her nearness. He'd made love to her for hours today, using their bond to store much-needed reserves for the battle ahead. Every time she climaxed, magic burst through him, enhancing and doubling before returning to her, creating a cycle that made them feel invincible together.

"But we aren't invincible," she argued against his unspoken

thoughts. "And I can't lose you. Your life isn't worth the risk. I can survive in a world with the Triumvirate. I can't survive in a world without you."

"This is what you wanted."

"Not anymore." Her lush mouth thinned with determination. She was so beautiful, her eyes a brilliant green surrounded by thick, ebony lashes. "For a long time, my desire for vengeance was the only thing I had in my life. My only reason for living. You've changed that, Max."

His hand pushed into the super-short strands of her hair and cupped the back of her head. "Tonight is our best chance to vanquish the Triumvirate for the entire year."

The world was filled with joy and love, with celebration and happiness, with the prayers of the believers and the hope of the nonbelievers. Mortals felt the change, although they didn't understand how real it was. The Triumvirate's powers would be diminished, a tiny advantage Max and Victoria desperately needed.

"Forget this year, and the next," she said with tears in her eyes. "Don't you see? I love you too much. Vanquishing the Triumvirate won't bring Darius back, and even if it could, it still wouldn't be worth it. That part of my life is over. You and I have a new life together, and it's more precious to me than anything."

"Kitten." Max's throat clenched tight. He hadn't thought it possible to love her more than he did, but the sudden ache in his chest proved him wrong. For centuries she'd sought a way to avenge Darius. Now she was willing to give up that quest. For him.

"How touching."

The grating voices of the Triumvirate swirled around them, rattling the protective bubble that shielded them from the snow. The force required to affect their warding spell was enormous, and Max inhaled sharply as Victoria was prompted to add her strength to his.

A shiver coursed down the length of her tense frame. Max felt it and soothed her with his touch, stroking along the curve of her spine.

"We can do this," he murmured, grimly determined.

Her hands fisted in his shirt. "Yes."

Max pressed a quick hard kiss to her forehead. She released him and took a place beside him, her fingers linking with his.

Before them in a line stood three hooded figures, their eyes glowing red from within the shadows of their cowls, their height well over seven feet tall, their frames rail thin but possessed of phenomenal power.

"Perhaps we'll take you this time, pretty kitty," one rasped at Victoria, laughing. His face was white as chalk and heavily lined, as if the skin were slowly melting off the underlayer of bones.

"Not on my life," Max challenged softly.

"Of course not," another cackled. "What would be the fun otherwise?"

The Triumvirate's unified front and appearance magnified the feeling that one faced a veritable army when they opposed them. While other demons and hellhounds were routinely discarded and removed from the Source's favor, these brethren had been immutable in the Order of Evil for centuries. Most magickind had come to see them as a fixture as permanent as Satan. They simply were and would always be.

In a lightning-quick movement, Victoria crouched and extended her arm, expelling a fiery ball of magic to hit the brother in the center. Almost instantly, two retaliatory strikes shot toward her from the left and right, the strength of the blows enough to rock her back on her feet despite the wards around her.

Max lunged forward, both hands out, returning fire. Victoria again attacked the one in the middle, resulting in the Triumvirate taking simultaneous hits.

If not for Darius's gift to her, Victoria would be unable to do more than stand beside Max and strengthen him, as she'd done the night Darius had been killed. But now she carried the strength of the fallen warlock inside her. Darius's power thrummed through her blood and enabled her to fight like a witch with Familiar augmentation. Max hoped that would be enough to save them both.

The Triumvirate retaliated as one, advancing one step at a time, sending volley after volley of ice-cold black magic to batter Max and Victoria's defenses.

But they did not retreat. As they struggled to keep the wards in place and return fire, sweat dotted their brows despite the raging blizzard. The Triumvirate howled their fury, seemingly unaffected by the assault against them.

Victoria glanced at Max, saw the set of his jaw and the corded veins in his temples as he poured gray magic out of his fingertips in crackling arcs of energy. He focused on one brother, his shoulders curling inward with the force with which he projected the power inside him.

As the insidious streams penetrated dark robes and charred moon-pale skin, the targeted brother screamed in agony. His siblings rushed to his aid, concentrating their attention on Max. Victoria continued to attack in the hopes of attracting fire in her direction. But in the face of the possible loss of one, the Triumvirate took her hits with admirable resilience.

The wards around Max began to ripple and bend, bowing to the greater might levered against the exterior. Blood trickled from one of his nostrils and his pain invaded her chest like a white-hot spear. Victoria wept, her stomach clenching with mindless terror. Memories of the night she'd lost Darius mingled with the horror of the present moment, creating a nightmare unparalleled.

The Triumvirate was too strong. Max would die.

Victoria screamed, unable to bear losing him.

Centuries alone . . . Afflicted by grief . . . Then Max had entered her life. Changing everything. Changing her. Making her whole again. Soothing her restlessness. Loving her despite her faults.

How will I live without you?

Then, with alarming swiftness, a solution presented itself in her mind, offering a slender ray of hope.

She could repeat the spell Darius had used, transferring the bulk of her power to Max. He would be stronger then, able to save himself and get away.

Do it.

Summoning every drop of magic she possessed, Victoria began to incant the spell she'd never forgotten. Could never forget because they'd been the last words Darius had spoken.

Pulled by an invisible thread, her power drew up and gathered, the sensation dizzying in its strength and strangeness. Her lips moved faster, the words flowing more freely.

"Victoria!" Max yelled, his shields moving sinuously in a herald to their rapidly approaching destruction.

It was her fault he was here, fighting a battle that was hers alone. It was love for her that had brought him to this end. It would be her love for him that would spare him.

"Max." Magic burst from Victoria in an explosion so powerful it brought her to her knees. It hit Max with such violence his body jerked as if physically struck. His wards restored to their rigid state and his bending arms straightened with renewed strength.

She gave all that she had to him, saving nothing for herself because her life would mean little without him. She wouldn't survive his loss. She'd barely survived Darius.

Max roared in triumph at the sudden, heady rush. A thin layer of warding separated from the one that shielded Max. It grew in size, expanding outward, encompassing the Triumvirate and preventing reinforcing power from the Source from reaching the brothers.

Unable to recharge his depleting strength, Max's target fell to his knees, crying out at his impending vanquishing.

Victoria watched through tear-filled eyes.

The Triumvirate draws strength from their numbers.

Darius's voice drifted through her mind. She and Max weren't alone. There were three of them, just as there were three of the brothers. And it was Christmas Eve. They had a fighting chance.

Using the very last of her strength, she sent one last volley toward the nearest brother. The impotent force of the blast was barely enough to draw his attention. But as she sank to her knees, his laser-bright gaze locked fully on her. She felt the satisfaction that gripped him at the sight of her weakened state. He would assume her support of Max was affecting her. He didn't know it was already too late.

Steeled for the inevitable blow, Victoria made no sound when the piercing evil of his strike sank deep into her chest, chilling her heart and slowing its beat. She bit her lip and fell to her hands, holding back any cry that might distract Max at the moment of triumph.

The alley began to spin and writhe. Another punishing blast struck her full on the crown of her head, knocking her to her back. Her skull thudded against the gritty, potted asphalt, and her sight dimmed and narrowed. Her ears rang, drowning out the sound of her racing pulse.

"Max . . . ," she whispered, tasting the coppery flavor of blood on her tongue.

A blinding explosion of light turned the night into day. Sulfur filled her nostrils and burned her throat. The buildings around them shook with the impact, freeing a cloud of minute debris that mingled with the falling snow.

You did it, my love, she thought as her limbs chilled.

"Victoria, no!"

Max's agonized cry broke her heart.

Icy snowdrops mingled with hot tears. In the sudden stillness, the distant sounds of Christmas songs and jingling bells tried to spread cheer. Instead it was a mournful requiem.

Her chest rose on a last breath.

I love you.

With Max on her mind and in her heart, Victoria died.

Two

Six hours earlier . . .

He was there, in the darkness. Watching her. Circling her.

His hunger wrapped around her, sharp and biting. Insatiable. It startled her sometimes, how ravenous he was. She could not temper or appease his desires.

She could only surrender. Submit. To them, to him.

Arching her back, her arms stretched the distance allowed by the silken bonds at her wrists, and her eyelids fluttered behind the red satin blindfold. Victoria stood, anchored, spread-eagled, her hands fisted around the forest green velvet ropes that extended from the ceiling. The colors of the season. More than mere sentimentality, it was a testament to Max's attention to detail. The same intense attention he paid to her body. He knew her inside and out, every curve and crevice, every dream and secret.

The sudden sharp smack of the crop against her bare buttocks made her hiss like the feline she was. The sting lingered, grew hot, made her writhe.

"Don't move, kitten," Max rumbled, his deep voice a husky caress.

If only she could see him. Her feline sight could drink him in, worship him. He was so beautiful. So delicious. Her warlock. Hers.

His lust was a potent scent in the air, dark and alluring, powerful. It beaded her nipples, swelled her breasts, slicked her sex. Her mouth watered for the taste of his cock and she purred, the low rumble an unmistakable plea for more. Always more.

She was as insatiable as he, driven by a love so consuming and vital she wondered how she'd ever lived without it.

"Max," she whispered, licking her lips. "I need you inside me."

Magic rose in the air between them, his considerable power augmented by her Familiar gifts. Her collar tingled around her neck. It was invisible to mortals, but to other magickind it was a blatant and unmistakable symbol of Max's ownership. A simple black ribbon that proclaimed she was owned, loved, looked after, protected. She'd rejected that symbol of submission for centuries after Darius had perished. Then Max Westin hunted her, and she learned to love supplication.

Now they were rogues, tasked with only the most unwanted assignments, punished by the Council at every turn. The adversity only made their bond stronger, deepening their connection.

"I love you," she breathed, arching in an effort to relieve the agonizing lust that consumed her. Her skin was hot and misted with sweat, desperate for the feel of his powerful body pressed to hers.

The scorching lash of a tongue on her beaded nipple made her cry out in near mindless longing.

"I love you, too," he murmured, his breath humid against her newly dampened skin. She heard the crop clatter on the floor just before his large hands cupped her hips.

"Y-yes." She swallowed hard. "Yes, Max."

As his heated face pressed into the valley between her breasts, his hands slid around to cup her buttocks, his fingers kneading into the firm flesh. His touch was gentle and reverent, despite the savage need she smelled on him. He loved her so much, enough to temper his passion and control it. There was nothing in the world like being made love to with such ferocious intensity and focus. Victoria was addicted to the pleasure he bestowed with such expert detail.

"Fuck me," she whispered through dry lips. "Gods, Max . . . I need your cock."

"Not yet, kitten. I'm not done playing."

She shuddered as his hot mouth wrapped around the aching tip of her breast. Panting, she writhed in his arms. "Damn you . . . you're killing me."

The sound of the Boston Pops playing holiday songs flowed in from the living room stereo, mingling with the sound of rushing blood in her ears. Outside, the snow continued to fall unabated, blanketing the city in a pristine layer. It was beautiful, but deceptive. The hair on Victoria's nape rose and a trickle of sweat coursed down her temple. Dark, insidious magic lay in wait for them. The whistling of the wind against the windows gave proof of that.

We're waiting, it whispered.

The sneering challenge of the Triumvirate given voice by the storm.

But here inside Max's vast loft apartment, she was shielded in a cocoon of desire and love. Together, their magic was a powerful force to be reckoned with. So far, they were undefeated. But they had never battled against any demon as close to the Source as the Triumvirate.

Think about me, Max snarled, his fingers tightening on her delicate skin.

His words echoed through her mind, a manifestation of the soul-deep connection between Master and Familiar. Their tie had to be at its strongest, its deepest, if they had any hope of succeeding tonight.

Always, she husked, wrapping her long legs around his lean waist. "It's always you."

She was lifted by his power, raised high into the air as if supported by a harness. The blindfold fell away, leaving her blinking, her sight adjusting into the feline night vision that allowed her to see her lover in all his glory.

Max stood between her spread thighs, his dark hair dampened by sweat and clinging to his arrogant brow. His eyes were dark and shining, his skin golden, his musculature made visible by sharp sexual tension.

As his head lowered and his lips approached her quivering cleft, the depth of his desire flooded her mind in a ferocious growl that made her jolt within her bonds.

My beautiful kitty has a beautiful pussy, he crooned. *Soft, sweet, and delicious.*

Then his mouth was between her legs, his tongue slipping through the slick folds and stroking across her swollen clitoris. She arched into his grip, her body shivering with the delightful torment.

With dazed, heavy-lidded eyes, Victoria took in the view of a gorgeous man eating her out with helpless fascination. Their love only added to the eroticism of the moment. Max relished having her this way, craving the taste of her so strongly that he sucked her off daily, his enjoyment obvious in the hungry snarls that vibrated against her tender flesh. His pleasure spurred hers until it rode her hard, tearing her apart.

Her power rose with the ecstasy he dispensed with wicked skill, augmenting his, filling the loft until the wooden ceiling beams and floorboards creaked with the effort to contain it.

"Let me touch you," she begged, her hands clenching and releasing restlessly. She could free herself easily, but she didn't. That made her submission even more valuable to him. He cherished her because of it, and she adored him for seeing it as the strength it was and not a weakness.

I want you like this.

She gasped as his lips circled her clitoris and he sucked, the pleasure radiating through her body in rolling waves. His tongue stroked rhythmically across the hardened bundle of nerves, making her pussy clench desperately in a silent plea to be filled.

"Max . . ."

His head tilted and he lifted her higher, his tongue thrusting deep, fucking hard and fast into the melting, spasming depths of her.

Victoria keened, coming hard, her back bowing as the orgasm stole her sight. Magic exploded from her like ripples on water, pouring into Max until he shook as savagely as she did.

But he didn't stop.

His lips, tongue, and teeth continued to feast on her, groans spilling from his throat as he drank her down. The silky curtain of his hair brushed against her inner thighs, adding to the overwhelming barrage of sensation that assailed her. It would all be too much if not for his love, which anchored her in the maelstrom and prevented her from losing her mind.

"Oh gods, Max," she whimpered, shivering with the aftershocks.

She'd never known sex could be so . . . *fervent* until she met Max. He took her body to places she hadn't known it could go. He allowed no barriers between them, no resistance.

Max released her wrists and she sank limply into his arms, her cheek falling to his shoulder and her lips touching his skin. The taste of him was an aphrodisiac, keeping her hot and wet. Hungry.

He set her carefully on her feet, then applied gentle but insistent pressure to her shoulders. "Suck my cock, kitten."

She sank gracefully and gratefully to her knees, her mouth watering for the taste of him and the feel of that heavy, vein-lined shaft sliding over her tongue. She was desperate for it, her throat clenching in anticipation.

He held the weighty length in one tightfisted hand and guided the flushed, glistening head to her parted lips.

"Yeah," he groaned, his chest heaving. "You look so beautiful when you're giving me head, baby."

Hot and throbbing, Max's cock slid inexorably into her drenched mouth. Her hands cupped his buttocks and drew him closer, her throat working to swallow and lure him deeper.

He kept one hand fisted around the base so he didn't feed her too much. The other hand cupped her cheek, feeling her mouth worshiping his cock from the outside.

"Gods," he gasped, his buttocks clenching against her palms as her tongue fluttered over the sensitive spot beneath the crown. "Slow down, kitten."

Victoria pulled free with a wet pop, her lips curving in a cat-like smile. Tilting her head, she followed a throbbing vein with the tip of her tongue, then circled his grasping hand. She backtracked, sucking softly as she moved upward, her emotions entangled with her physical responses.

"Fuck," he growled, his thighs quaking. "Suck it, baby. Don't play."

Pressing her lips to the tiny hole at the tip, she barely parted them, then flowed over him in a rapid dip of her head.

His hand left her cheek and cupped the back of her head, holding her still as he fucked her mouth in rapid, shallow digs. She moaned in delight, her thighs squeezed tightly together to fight the ache of emptiness in her pussy.

"Suck it hard, kitten."

Her cheeks hollowed on a drawing pull and his fierce shout of triumph swelled upward through the exposed ductwork, combating the sounds of the Triumvirate's challenge in the wind outside.

Shuddering, he spurted hot and thick, the creamy wash of his semen flowing over her tongue and down her throat. His fist stroked from the thick base of his cock to meet her lips, pumping his cum hard and fast along the jerking shaft into her waiting, willing mouth.

The power she'd given him with her climax flowed back into her, hotter and more powerful, a deluge so intense she wouldn't have been able to take it if not for the gift Darius gave her. She felt Max in her mind, his love flowing through her in a saturating embrace, his pleasure as necessary to her as breathing.

He pulled free of her suckling. The next instant cool, crushed velvet cushioned her back and Max was over her, kneeing her legs wider so his hips could sink between them. She purred at the feel of the slick head of his cock notching into place at the tiny slitted entrance of her pussy.

With a powerful lunge, he was deep inside her, his still-rigid cock thrusting through her swollen tissues until he'd hit the end of her.

"Max!" His name was a breathless cry on her lips, her toes curling with the delight of having him pulsing within her, stretching her to her limits in the most delicious way possible.

"Naughty kitten," he rumbled, nuzzling his cheek against hers. "You almost finished me with your mouth."

"I love your cock, Max."

"As much as you can take." His head lifted and his gaze promised hours of joy ahead of her. "I'll always give you as much as you can handle, kitten."

"Give it to me now," she purred. "Hard and deep."

Fists clenched in the coverlet, Max obliged her, pounding

her into the mattress with the heated length of his magnificent cock. He whispered lewd praise in her ear, describing how she felt around him, how he loved her hot pussy and greedy cries for more.

Victoria clawed at his back, her long legs wrapping around his pumping hips, her pussy tightening on every withdraw and quivering on every plunge. Gluttonously relishing the brutality of his passion.

There was a desperation in his taking, a primal urge to sink as deep into her as possible so that they could never be separated. They faced the greatest foe of their lives tonight and they might not survive it.

I love you . . . so beautiful . . . mine . . .

As his emotions filled her mind and heart, tears coursed down her temples to wet her hair. She embraced his sweat-slick back and spread her legs wider, sobbing with the mind-numbing pleasure of his possession, trembling violently from an orgasm more fierce than anything she'd ever experienced before.

His climax followed hers, his cum spurting in scorching skeins, his cock jerking inside her with every wrenching pulse. Their combined magic swelled, shaking every item in the loft. The windows creaked, whined, barely able to contain the power they created as one. On this night.

Victoria clung to Max, crying. She wouldn't lose him. She couldn't.

If the end approached, it would be her life for his.

She would ensure it.

Three

Midnight, the witching hour

He was going to die.

The hot trickle of blood from Max's nostril assured him of that fact. His veins felt scorched by acid, his chest burned with every gasping breath, his skull felt as if it were being squeezed in a vise. Every blow to his warding spell felt like a physical one and they were incessant, coming from two sides.

"Victoria!" Max yelled, his shields rippling sinuously in testament to their swiftly approaching collapse. She had to turn and flee, before his strength waned and left her vulnerable.

Run!

Just as his vision began to dim and he feared slipping into unconsciousness, a surge of power almost too potent to contain tore through him in a scalding rush.

Victoria. So visceral it felt as if her very soul had entered his body. Her augmentation whipped around and through him, strengthening and protecting him from harm.

As his target sank to his knees and victory was at hand, an invasive chill spread outward from the center of Max's chest and gripped his heart. The icy fist tightened, then spread insidiously through his veins. The sudden dearth of Victoria in his mind was like a scream in silence, piercing and terrifying.

Turning his head, he looked for her and found her sprawled on the pavement, a smoldering hole in her beautiful chest.

"Victoria, NO!"

Her beloved voice with its soft, throaty purr whispered through his mind. *I love you.*

Max roared into the storm. His hands began to lower, his need to be with her a driving impulse that he couldn't deny.

But she wouldn't allow him to give up.

Her strength of will straightened his arms and increased the flow of gray magic he sent into the falling brother. His quivering arms shot forward and magic poured from the tips of his fingers in white-hot streams, arcing through the air like lightning, sinking deep into the collapsing body of the middle Triumvirate brother. The wards around him thickened, shielding him from the blows that pelted his frontal perimeter.

His body and magic were no longer his own. They were possessed by a force greater than himself. Something strange and new penetrated deep into his bones, embracing his grief and fury. Magnifying them and sending them outward in a shockwave of power so destructive it shattered his wards and sliced through the center of the Triumvirate brethren like a guillotine blade.

Their screams echoed through the alley, rising like banshees' cries, ripping apart the sky in a thunderous boom. As one, the Triumvirate exploded in a blinding flash, rocking Max back on his heels and quaking the very ground beneath him. The buildings shook with such violence they threatened to topple, and animals across the city protested in a sudden cacophony. Dogs whined and howled. Cats screeched. Birds fled their warm nests in a riot of flapping wings and caws.

Then the alley fell silent. The only sounds that broke the stillness were the jingling of distant sleigh bells and Max's own tortured sobbing.

He dropped to the snow on his knees, the emptiness inside him a gaping, yawning hole he knew he couldn't survive. He needed Victoria. Couldn't live without her.

Centuries he'd spent alone, focused on his primary mission—enforcing the will of the Council by death. Victoria had brought light into his life, warmth with the heat of her passion, and love into the emptiness of his heart.

"Damn you," he said hoarsely, crawling toward her as debris rattled down and mingled with the snowflakes. "You can't leave me here alone."

Max caught her up and pulled her into his lap. Chanting one spell after another. Trying everything he knew, black and white magic, *anything* at all to heal her and bring her back to him.

But she didn't move, her chest did not rise and fall with breath, her eyelids didn't flutter over the brilliant emerald irises he adored.

"Kitten . . . ," he sobbed. "You can't leave me here alone . . . you can't leave me . . ."

Rocking her, Max pressed shaking lips to her forehead

and felt his sanity slipping from him like sands through an hourglass.

"Heal her!" His command cracked through the night, reaching out to the Council who heard and saw everything. "Heal her or I will hunt you down," he hissed. "Every last one of you. I'll kill you all. I swear it."

We told you this would happen, They crowed. *Her loss is the penalty for your arrogance.*

Max's jaw tightened. His gaze narrowed on Victoria, who looked beautiful and oddly peaceful. Her skin pale and luminous like a pearl, her thick lashes spiked from tears and melting snow. She glowed. Softly, faintly. With an inner radiance.

Stilling, Max took in that hint of illumination. And what it signified.

The magic within her still lived. Darius's magic.

You can't have her, Max growled, fury overtaking his crushing grief. *She's mine.*

There were consequences for penetrating the Transcendual Realm. Dire penalties.

He didn't care.

He would be stained, marked. Some would hunt him as a rogue. Peace would be ephemeral with a price on his head.

Max didn't hesitate. It would all be worth it. *If* he had Victoria.

Slicing across his wrist with a sliver of magic, he held his arm above the wounds in Victoria's chest. The crimson of his blood blended with the snow and dripped onto her charred flesh. The mixture sizzled atop her skin and smoke rose.

Max closed his eyes and began to incant.

• • •

Victoria woke with a gasp and found herself lying in a field of yellow flowers. The air was redolent of lilies and sun-warmed grass, and butterflies flitted through the air in rarely seen numbers.

Pushing up to a seated position, she perused her surroundings with greater care, attempting to reconcile the beauty of the summer day with the snow-covered alley she'd occupied just a moment before. She looked down, noting the simple linen shift she wore, cleanly cut and unadorned. Her hand lifted to her unmarred chest and she frowned.

Where was Max? And where was she?

A masculine hand penetrated her vision.

Her gaze lifted and came to rest on a beloved face she thought she would never see again.

"Darius."

"Hello, Vicky." His beautiful mouth curved in a loving smile. The sunlight lit his golden hair with a luminousness that stole her breath and tightened her chest. Her favorite dimple dotted his cheek and brought back a flood of treasured memories.

"Where are we?"

She accepted the hand he held out to her, allowing him to pull her to her feet.

"Together," he said simply. "Although I've always been with you."

Darius linked his fingers with hers. "Walk with me?"

"Am I dead?"

His head tilted to the side, as if listening to something she couldn't hear. His handsome features took on a thoughtful cast and his lips pursed. Then he set off, pulling her along with him, forgetting to answer her. Or choosing not to.

As they strolled, recognition of their location came to her—the south of France. One of the many places they'd visited and enjoyed as a couple.

"Have you been here the whole time?" she asked.

"No. I switch it up every now and then."

"'Switch it up'?"

He glanced aside at her with a familiar twinkle in his eye. "I'm keeping up with vernacular."

As flowers crushed beneath their feet, sweetly alluring fragrances filled the air. It was paradise, in a fashion, but echoes of pain and longing turned down the corners of her mouth.

Max. Her fear for him was paramount in her mind.

"Where are we, Darius?"

"You know where we are." He looked straight ahead, revealing no more than the classical elegance of his profile.

"Is it over for me, then?"

"It can be." With a gesture of his hand, he directed her to sit upon a half-moon bench that hugged a tree. A tree that had not been there just a second ago.

"You still have magic," she said.

"It is ingrained in us."

Victoria sat, her fingers moving restlessly over the edge of her skirt. The urgency inside her grew with every breath she took, sparking a driving need to act. For her, the clock was ticking double time, a jarring contrast to the pervasive leisure she felt in the Transcendual Realm.

Darius sat beside her and picked up one of her hands in his. "When I first saw you," he said softly, "I knew you were the only woman for me. The sensation was lightning in a bottle, an instantaneous awareness. I was certain, prior to exchanging a word with you, that you would make me happier than I had ever been or could ever be without you."

Her eyes stung as her vision blurred with tears. "I felt the same."

"I always knew you loved me."

"Yes . . ."

"I also knew that I was not your soul mate."

Victoria stilled. Darius smiled, but his handsome features were marred by sorrow.

"What are you saying?"

"You were all I needed, Vicky, but I couldn't be all you needed. I didn't have a firm enough hand. You were content with me, but not thriving."

"No," she protested, canting to face him directly. "That's not true."

"It is." He cupped her cheek, his thumb following the line of her cheekbone. "That's why I gifted my power to you. I wanted you to have a choice. I wanted to give you the opportunity to get it right the next time."

"It was right the first time," she insisted. "I will always care for you, always love you."

"I know." The sadness left his blue eyes, replaced by the mischievous twinkle she'd fallen in love with. "What we had was perfect . . . but now you have something even more perfect. I wish I could have been that for you. Still, I'm grateful for what we did have. I know we had something wonderful."

"Yes. We did." Victoria glanced at the field of flowers around them. "What happens now?"

"Now, you decide." He squeezed her hand. "Stay with me or live the rest of your eight lives."

She bumped his shoulder with hers. "That's a myth."

Darius grinned. "Is it?" he teased, standing.

Victoria rose to her feet and stared up at him. "Are you happy?"

"Of course." His dimple flashed. "I'm with you always. There's nothing more I could ask for."

"Do you want me to stay?"

"I want you to be happy," he said, in a low ardent tone. "Whether that's with me or with Westin. He loves you. Almost as much as I do. He's fighting to bring you back as we speak."

"I love him." Her tears flowed freely.

"I'm glad, Vicky."

"I love you, too."

"I know you do."

His golden head lowered, bringing his mouth to hers. His advance was slow, yet heartrendingly familiar. The press of his lips soothed a long restless part of her heart. She hadn't had the chance to say good-bye; he'd been ripped from her too quickly. That lack of closure had haunted her for centuries.

Victoria's hands fisted in Darius's linen shirt and she kissed him desperately. Not with the passion she felt for Max, but with the lingering love they'd once shared. It was a bittersweet parting, but one that felt absolutely right. Her life was with Max now. So was her heart.

"Thank you," she whispered. "I couldn't have saved him without you."

"I'll see you on the flip side, love," Darius replied softly. "Stay out of trouble until then."

She tried to open her eyes, but sank into darkness instead.

• • •

Victoria woke to the feel of snow falling on her face. Warmth cradled her right side and she rolled into it, groaning as searing agony burned through her chest.

"Kitten?" Even from a perceived distance, the aching wonder in Max's voice could not be mistaken.

"Hi." She pressed her cheek to his soaked shirt. "Miss me?"

"Don't tease, damn you. I could kill you for putting me through that." He caught her close, his large frame quaking with the violence of his emotions. "What a shitty stunt to pull on a man. Especially on Christmas."

"I'm sorry, baby." Her hand curled around his side.

Take good care of her, Westin.

Darius's voice moved through her like a tangible caress.

"I will," Max assured hoarsely.

Turning her head, Victoria found Darius standing a few feet away. Translucent and glowing, he watched her with warm, loving eyes.

Live for yourself now, he admonished gently. *You've lived enough centuries for me.*

She nodded.

With a wave, he was gone.

And with a snapping of Max's fingers, so were Victoria and Max.

Epilogue

Six days later . . .

"If you ever do that again," Max growled, rising over her in his velvet-covered bed, "I'll spank your ass red."

"Is that supposed to be a threat?"

She purred as he rolled his hips and pushed his magnificent cock into her.

"Kitten, you have no idea." He withdrew and thrust deep, the wide-flared head of his cock stroking across a sensitive spot inside her. "I thought I was losing my mind in that alley. I would have, if Darius hadn't brought you back to me."

"I'll always come for you, Max."

Holding her hip with one hand, he responded to her teasing by shafting her pussy in hard, fierce drives. "Come for me now," he bit out.

She climaxed with a mewl, gasping as heated pleasure exploded across her senses with dazzling brightness.

An edgy rumble vibrated in his chest. "Fuck, that sound makes me hot as hell."

"After nearly a week of nothing but showers, food, and sex?" she asked breathlessly. "You're insatiable."

"I'm just enjoying my Christmas present, kitten. Besides, you love it."

Max stared down at her with his stormy gray eyes and she knew she'd never loved him more. He'd kept her within touching distance for the last week; cooking her favorite meals, feeding her by hand, and washing her hair and body. For a Familiar, it was heaven, and she soaked it up like sunshine after a long, dreary winter.

"Max . . ."

He thrust rhythmically, plunging deep and slow to give her time to recover, making her feel every throbbing inch of him.

Her neck arched, her nails dug into his back, and her pussy fluttered in helpless delight around him.

"Oh yeah," he rumbled, a wicked smile curving one side of his gorgeous mouth. "You definitely love it."

"I love you." She offered her mouth and he took it with breathtaking passion.

"I love you back."

Finally content, Victoria's lips curved against his in a catlike smile.

Black Magic

Woman

One

*M*ax Westin stood in the coffee shop across the street from the St. John Hotel and barely tempered his anticipation for the orgasms he'd be relishing in the hours ahead.

The woman who would be serving his needs was already inside. He'd watched Victoria greet her morning business appointment at the curb, her lithe body encased in a black pencil skirt and emerald silk blouse that perfectly matched her sloe eyes. She'd been wearing nude stilettos, making her already long legs appear endless.

He couldn't wait to feel them wrapped around his hips, tightening in a vain effort to hold his thrusting cock inside her.

The barista called out his name and he went to the counter to collect Victoria's favorite tea, which he'd ordered liberally laced with heavy cream. As he exited to the street, he checked his watch, noting that he would be exactly on time to use lunch as an excuse to monopolize her attentions. His blood thrummed through his veins, heating with every step he took.

He'd been gone for two days on a High Council summons and he felt the withdrawals of separation acutely. His dick was thick and heavy between his legs, his balls full and tight. The need to come in the tight, plush depths of Victoria's honey-sweet cunt rode him hard.

Max entered the St. John through the revolving lobby door and nodded at the three employees manning the front desk. If he'd been certain Victoria's morning meeting was over, he could've bridged the distance between them in the blink of an eye, an embarrassingly simple spell for a warlock of his power. Instead, he rounded the corner to step into the private passcoded elevator.

As the car began its ascent, he forcibly reined in his desire. His endless hunger for his mate had been sharpened by the black magic that shrouded his latest hunt. Although Victoria was more than strong enough to sate his darkest cravings, he wanted to greet her with tenderness. He wanted to show her that he'd missed her from the very depths of his soul—because he'd begun a hunt without her and knew that would hurt her, despite the validity of his reasons for doing so.

The moment the elevator doors opened on the executive level, he saw her. His chest tightened with the ferocity of his love for her, the fierce sense of connection he'd only ever felt with her. She stood in the reception area of her office, one hand on a slim hip and a wide smile on her stunning face. She spoke to the two men Max had seen with her on the street, and their avid gazes betrayed their heated masculine appreciation. The men were enchanted by her beauty and mischievous nature, as all males were, and she was toying with them like the cat she was.

Max gestured for her secretary to remain quiet so he could enjoy the show, but Victoria felt him, felt the charge of power that surged between them and the inner serenity that came from being rejoined with the other half of one's self. She glanced at him, and he could almost see her swish her tail.

"Ah, gentlemen," she purred. "You'll have to excuse me now. My lunch date is here."

The two suits looked at him then, sizing him up.

"Don't let me rush you," Max told her. "I can wait."

"*I* can't." She came to him and took the cup from his hand. "My favorite tea. Thank you. Why don't you make yourself comfortable in my office? I won't be but a moment."

He moved to do as she asked, his hand brushing affectionately and proprietarily over the curve of her hip.

Victoria's office had walls of windows on two sides—one overlooking the bustling city below and the other facing the reception area. It was a feminine space that still conveyed power, and it was where she ran a hospitality empire. Her quick and clever mind kept her a few steps ahead of her competition, while her feline sensibilities assured comfort, luxury, and unobtrusive service for her clientele.

Unbuttoning the jacket of his Armani suit, Max shrugged out of it and tossed it over the back of a chair facing her desk.

Before he'd ever met her, he had admired her intelligence and ambition. In the time they'd been together, his respect and appreciation had only deepened. Being here, in her lair, reinforced his pride in her accomplishments. He knew damn well how fortunate he was to be the man who laid claim to her. It was a decision he'd make again if given the choice, even knowing what it would cost him and all he would risk to share his life with such a magnificent woman.

She entered the office in a rush, her eyes bright with love and pleasure at the sight of him. Her glossy raven hair was shorn close to her scalp, to better showcase her slender neck and sculpted cheekbones. That luxurious pelt remained unchanged in her feline form along with her eyes. In either incarnation—woman or Familiar—she took his breath away.

Love for her lengthened his cock and goaded every primal instinct he possessed. She'd been close to feral when they first met. His assignment had been to either tame her for eventual pairing with another warlock or vanquish her. In the end, he could do nothing but keep her for himself. She'd become as necessary to him as the air he breathed. The shadows of wildness in her perfectly suited his tendency to skirt the edges of black magic.

Kicking the door shut behind her, Victoria crossed the expansive room with her lush feline grace. "I've missed you like crazy, Max."

"No more than I've missed you." He wrapped her throat with his hands, mimicking the collar that bound her to him. With a thought, he set a glamour on the wall of windows framing her office door, shielding their embrace from view of the reception area and creating a compulsion to avoid disturbing them.

He was home. *She* was his home.

Max took her mouth in lush hot kiss, his tongue thrusting deep and sure, sliding along hers. His grip tightened, not enough to cut off her air, but enough to increase the feeling of pressure that would urge her mind away from work and into the place where just the two of them existed. Victoria moaned and melted into him, instantly shedding the weight of command and surrendering to his insatiable need for her. A wild joy filled him.

I love you. Her ardent declaration slid through his mind like fragrant smoke, chasing away the shadows that had steadily encroached on him over the last two days. Black magic was seductive, and hunting two consummate practitioners had re-awakened his craving for it. If not for Victoria's love, he might be vulnerable to its lure. She kept him sane and straight, anchoring him as his power continued to grow with every day that passed.

His lips parted from hers and moved to her ear. "Were you good while I was gone?"

She clutched his waist. "Of course. But it was hard."

Pulling back, he looked at her. He rubbed his thumb over her full bottom lip, knowing how needy she must be after obeying his command not to pleasure herself while he was gone. "Not as hard as my dick has been the last two days. I was going to wait until after lunch, but I'll have your mouth now, kitten."

She nipped the pad of his thumb with her teeth, her eyes submissively downcast. He tugged her backward, keeping her with him until he reached the front of her desk and half sat on the edge.

"Touch me," he ordered, needing her hands on him.

She unbuttoned his vest with nimble fingers, parting the edges to run her hands down the length of his tie. "What did the High Council want?"

"What They always want." He took a deep breath, hesitating to ruin her happy mood. "Sirius Powell escaped."

Victoria stilled, her hand settling over his heart. Then she pulled a chair over and sat. "How is that possible?"

"He had help—Xander Barnes escaped with him."

Her hand went to her throat, feeling for the collar that only those who practiced magic could see. *His* collar—the symbol of her submission and his possession. Victoria understood the gravity of the news. Both Powell and Barnes were vicious rogues so addicted to black magic that they killed those who practiced it to steal their power.

She didn't ask him why They'd chosen him. She knew he was the Council's first choice for hunting Others—those who'd crossed over too far into black magic and couldn't be saved. Still, he elaborated, "I'm the one who captured them both to begin with."

Her hand dropped to her lap and curled into a fist. "Of course. Were they separate then? Or together?"

"Separate. But my orders are different this time. Now I just need to put them down."

"You said 'I' instead of 'we.'" Her gaze hardened. "We're a team, Max. You don't work alone anymore."

He cupped her face in his hands. As a Hunter of rogues, he shouldn't have a Familiar. While Familiars augmented a warlock or witch's power tremendously, they were also a terrible point of weakness in battle. He understood firsthand how true that was, because he'd very nearly lost Victoria in their fight against the Triumvirate. The sight of her bleeding and broken in the snow that night, her life slipping away even as he gripped her body close, had taken him to the brink of insanity.

But he would never give her up; he couldn't. He had forsaken everything he'd ever worked for, forfeiting a prized seat on the High Council and thereby inciting its members' wrath, because his life wasn't worth living without her in it.

"There's a reason Hunters don't have Familiars," he reminded gently. "Besides, this is unfinished business from before I met you."

"So was my fight against the Triumvirate," she shot back, "but I let you fight it with me. Don't you dare act like I'm a liability."

His fingertips followed the curve of her eyebrows. "You're my heart."

"Max." Her voice softened. But as she searched his face, her gaze narrowed and took on the calculating look of a clever feline.

To distract her and remind her of the command she had yet to obey, he waved a hand and stood before her naked, his clothes folded neatly on the sofa behind her. Sitting at eye level with his groin, Victoria licked her lips. She fought her need to obey for a moment, then conceded and reached for him, her slender hands circling his aching length.

Max's hands slid to her throat, tilting her chin up so that their gazes met. "You'll suck my cock because it pleases me, not because you see it as a way to manage me."

"Why can't it be for both reasons?" she challenged.

"Ah, Victoria," he crooned, his blood heating at a dangerous pace. With a focused thought, silken rope appeared and coiled sinuously around her wrists, binding them behind her back. "Let's occupy that pretty mouth of yours with something else before you get spanked."

"Max . . ." She trembled with excitement, her nipples hard beneath her blouse. As much as she liked control, she liked relinquishing it as well—to him. Him alone.

"On your knees," he murmured, stroking himself from root to tip.

She slid from the chair and lowered gracefully to the floor, her balance honed by her feline side.

He fisted his cock, stroking a stream of pre-cum to the tip. "Lick it off, kitten. With that hot, rough little tongue of yours."

Tilting her head back, she opened her mouth, moaning when he cupped the back of her head in one hand and slid his cock into her with the other.

"Deep and slow," he instructed.

Max watched her submit, a groan tearing from him at the feel of her. Her mouth flowed over him, surrounding the sensitive crown in a wash of wet heat. His head bowed forward, his gaze slitting as his eyelids became weighted with drugging desire. He touched her hair, running his fingers through the short cap of silky strands, trying to convey without words how much he treasured her.

Then she sucked, pulling him deeper, and his body stiffened as the pleasure threatened to destroy the reins of his control.

He groaned, his dick so hard it ached. "You suck me so good. There's nothing in the world like fucking your greedy little mouth."

Her wicked tongue fluttered across the underside of his cock head and sweat broke out on his chest. She watched him with those tip-tilted green eyes, her love burning hotly, her awareness of her feminine power shining in the emerald depths. The tip of her tongue probed the hole at the head of his cock, lapping up the pre-cum that flowed in a steady stream.

"Gods, you're beautiful . . ." He shuddered as she nuzzled his balls with her cheek. They were already high and tight, heavy with semen desperate to spurt down her working throat. She took a deep, drawing pull on the tender crest, milking him. She swallowed greedily, purring, eliciting another wash of creamy cum.

She hummed her delight at the taste of him, sucking faster, tonguing the thick crest.

His hands fisted; one at his side, the other in her hair. His abdomen laced tight, his body fighting the need to come too quickly. Her mouth was so plush and hot, her desire so ravenous. The erotic sounds filling the room spurred his lust, pushed him closer to the edge of reason.

"You're killing me," he said gruffly, his chest tight with love for her. "Not too fast. Make it last."

She moaned around his cock as if she worshipped it, releasing him to kiss the tip before tracing the thick veins along the length with her tongue. The brutal pleasure battered at what little control he had after going days without her. Dark magic writhed inside him, struggling against the emotions Victoria inspired. There was no room for love in black magic. And no room for black magic in Max's bond with his beloved.

"Max," she breathed. "Don't hold back."

Angling his cock, he traced her lips with the tip. "I'll come for you," he promised roughly. "When it's time."

She pouted and he smiled grimly, knowing she thought he was teasing her. The truth wasn't as pretty, but similarly motivated by his concern for her. When he came, his magic would flow into her, become magnified by her Familiar gifts, and returned to him. She'd feel his turmoil then and understand where it came from.

She took him deep, her cheeks hollowing.

"Victoria."

Her tongue fluttered against the sensitive underside, teasing him, tempting him with the promise of an explosive climax.

Cupping her cheeks to hold her still, Max rocked his hips, fucking her eager little mouth at *his* pace. Sliding in and out, he allowed the pleasure to build until he felt the first tingles of orgasm. Then he slowed, savoring the rush.

"Gods," he growled, his legs weakened by the ferocious need to let go after days without her.

Victoria whimpered and sucked franticly, her tongue swirling. Her need to please him moved him, urged him to give her what she wanted. He released her and grasped for the desk, his hands curling around the edge.

She bobbed her head and took him to the back of her throat, again and again, her eyelids fluttering as she focused on finishing him. Her plush lips slid up and down his length, stroking him, coaxing cum into her working mouth. Sleepy-eyed, she stared up at him, her nipples straining, begging for his touch.

He cupped her tits in his hands, squeezing them, his thumbs circling over the tight points. She shivered and moaned, the vibration reverberating through his tightly strung frame. Her pheromones permeated the air, the scent so carnal and tantalizing he couldn't resist it.

With a gasp, he let go, coming. The first wrenching pulse jolted through him, molten heat racing down his spine before bursting from the tip of his cock. He growled as he spurted hotly, pumping semen across her flickering tongue. Her throat hugged him, closing on a deep swallow as she drank him down. Spots swam before his eyes, his lungs seizing as the orgasm shattered him. His power exploded from his taut frame in a surge of heat.

The lights flickered wildly. With a pained cry, Victoria absorbed the magic into her, then released it in a power surge that snapped the rope at her wrists and exploded the lightbulb in her desk lamp. Darkness hissed through the room, coiling and slithering, then slamming into Max and rocking him back into the desk.

Victoria stumbled up and into him, catching him and holding on. Max buried his damp face in the crook of her neck and crushed her to him, shuddering as the power pulsed through him like a viciously pounding headache.

Her fingers dug into his back. "Max . . . What have you done?"

Two

$\mathscr{X}$ander Barnes lifted his wineglass to his lips and looked through the restaurant's windows to the bistro patio across the street. There, Max Westin was hand-feeding tempting morsels to his beautiful Familiar. "We'll have to vanquish her," he thought aloud. "She's making him too strong. We'll never take him out while he has her."

"Hmm." Sirius Powell cut into his steak. "Before I saw them together, I would've agreed. But I've changed my mind. See the way he looks at her? He loves her. It would be a waste to excise such a weakness with a single strike."

Xander crossed his arms. A soft afternoon breeze rifled through his copper hair like a lover's fingers. "We'll have to use her against him, then."

"Yes. I think so."

"She has Darius Whitacre's power."

Sirius smiled and set down his utensils. The Familiar was

unique, thanks to her previous warlock who'd bequeathed her his power. That magic made her strong, which made Max Westin stronger, but it also created a novel vulnerability. "Whitacre's power makes her susceptible to black magic. We just need to give her the incentive to use it."

"Westin is already dabbling in it to lure us out. If she hasn't had a taste of it yet, she will soon enough."

"Which will give her a taste for more," Sirius finished. "Darius's magic isn't her only weakness. Westin is, too. Considering how territorial Familiars are, she won't want to be reminded about how many witches Westin has enjoyed."

Xander laughed softly. "You want to make a Familiar jealous? You are evil."

Sirius toyed with the long blond braid hanging over his shoulder. "And we'll get a great show. Who should we tap to get things rolling?"

"Jezebel Patridge," Xander said without hesitation. "She and Westin were hot and heavy for a while. When he was hunting me, I considered using her as leverage, but it didn't pan out."

"How do you propose getting her involved?"

Grinning, Xander leaned back in his chair and sipped his wine. "With a note from Westin himself. Easy enough to counterfeit."

Sirius lifted his own glass in toast. "This should be fun."

Something was wrong.

Victoria leaned into the threshold of the kitchen and watched as Max prepared dinner. From the first night he'd walked into her life with the High Council's order to either tame her or kill her, he'd been taking care of her. She'd never been so pampered and spoiled in her long life. In return Max expected nothing but her love, trust, and submission, all of which she gave him, despite her alpha female disposition.

Her adoring gaze took in every mouthwatering inch of him, from the top of his head to the tips of his toes. His inky-black hair hung to his shoulders in a thick luxurious mane, framing a face so savagely masculine it made her shiver just to look at him. His eyes were the gray of a summer storm and his lips were simply divine, so firm and beautifully sculpted.

His powerful arms and back flexed as he worked at the stove, his body unadorned except for a loose pair of silk pajama pants. His bare feet were a wicked enticement for her feline sensibilities, luring her to shift forms and twine around his ankles. His skin was the color of the richest caramel, the texture firm and satin soft. His taut ass made her mouth water, and when he turned toward the sink, she eyed the unmistakable sway of his heavy cock, her pussy clenching hungrily for the feel of him thrusting inside her.

The two days she'd spent without him had been torture enough, but the hours since lunch had been worse. A wall had gone up between them since they'd left her office. Knowing he was home but still distant was both physically and emotionally painful. He'd shut her out in a way he never had before. Although he was still affectionate and attentive, there was no doubt that he was shielding her from the truth of where he'd been the last two days and what he'd done. During lunch he'd talked about everything except what he had decided to do about the Council's summons.

Max had always been one to use gray magic. But what she'd felt today was much more dangerous. And far more seductive.

Even now she could feel the darkness shrouding his soul and the iron control he was exerting to contain it. The hunt for sorcerers of Sirius Powell and Xander Barnes's power would push him to the very edge. The assignment would tax his strength in myriad ways and it was up to her to support him through it. But she couldn't do that if he wouldn't let her in.

Untying her black silk robe, Victoria went to him and pressed her bared torso to his back, her arms wrapping around his chest. Her palms slid over his washboard abs and firm pectorals, squeezing the hot, hard flesh with greedy hands.

"I love you, Max," she murmured with her lips to his shoulder blade.

"I know, kitten."

She reached lower, cupping him through the silk of his pants, then loosening the drawstring to fist his thickening cock skin to skin. "I need you."

He swelled in her grasp, eliciting a purr of delight from her. Her nipples stiffened, her pussy softening in readiness. She stroked him from root to tip, making him longer and harder, priming him to pleasure her.

Abruptly, he turned off the burner and spun fluidly. He took control with breathtaking ease, catching her hands behind her with one of his own. Excitement flushed her skin.

Max loomed over her, his eyes stormy and hot. His free hand ran down the center of her body from throat to sex, possessively cupping the pulsing flesh between her legs. "What do you want, Victoria?"

"You." She spread her legs, inviting his touch. "I've always wanted you, from the moment you walked into my life."

Parting her, he gently rubbed her clit. "You've had me from the beginning."

Her entire body softened, her heart pounding at being restrained and pleasured. "I don't feel like I have you now."

He circled the clenching entrance to her body with skillful fingertips. "You own me."

She gasped as he lowered his head to lick across one peaked nipple, his tongue a velvet lash. "Why won't you talk to me about what's happened the last couple of days?"

His silky hair brushed over the curves of her breasts. His lips surrounded the aching point, his cheeks hollowing as he suckled her. Two fingers pushed inside her. "I missed you," he murmured against her damp skin. "I'd fuck you endlessly if I could, stay inside you forever. When I'm not in you, I'm thinking about it. Craving it. I don't feel whole when I'm not a part of you."

"Be a part of me now," she whispered, her hips circling onto his gently thrusting fingers. Fire raced across her skin, eliciting a mist of sweat. Her womb clenched with the depth of her need to be connected to him.

"I'm cooking now." His whisky-rough voice was low and firm, his fingers stilling . . . letting her feel him there, letting her crave the friction and heady rush of release. "When it's time to play, I'll tell you."

"Please, Max."

"Shhh. I'll take care of you." He curled his fingers and stroked over the tender spot inside her, over and over. She climaxed with a soft cry, quivering in his arms.

He gave her what she wanted without giving anything of himself away.

His lips brushed across her parted ones, her panting breaths gusting over his jaw. "Better?"

Victoria whimpered as his fingers left her. "No." Without his pleasure, she was empty. Unfulfilled. "You're shutting me out, Max."

His gaze slid over her face, so full of love and yet so guarded. "You have to trust me."

Her chest tightened painfully. "That's not fair."

"Come to terms with it, Victoria," he said with quiet authority.

"We've always worked together," she argued.

"And we will again, when the situation warrants it." He caught her chin in one hand. "Even with Darius's power, there are limits to what you can do. And augmenting my magic when going after two rogues like Sirius and Xander can backfire."

"Then let me support you at home! Talk to me. Don't leave me in the dark."

Max's hand slid beneath her robe to cup her bare buttock and drag her hard against him. "Let me take care of you. That's all I need."

His head lowered and he took her mouth, kissing her with the possessive passion that had seduced her from the first. His firm lips sealed over hers, his tongue gliding deep to stroke against her own. A growl rumbled in his chest and vibrated against her breasts, the light dusting of hair on his chest an unbearable stimulation. He was hard and thick, his erection pressing against her lower belly.

He ate at her mouth, possessing it, tasting her with long

deep licks. His fingers pushed into the short strands of her hair, cupping her scalp and holding her steady as he drank in her taste. His tongue fucked her leisurely, teasing her with the promise of what she truly wanted.

Victoria moaned, lost in him. Her lips felt swollen and hot, her eyelids heavy with the drugging effects of Max's skilled seduction. His fervent words echoed through her mind, his declarations of uncontrolled obsession in erotic contrast to his absolute control while handling her.

When she was breathless and pliant, he pulled away. Running his tongue along the kiss-plumped curve of her mouth, he murmured, "Dinner first."

Victoria nodded, but her mind raced. She'd already lost a man she loved once. She'd be damned if she would sit quietly while it happened again.

Three

*M*ax speared another slice of a bay scallop, swirled it in savory cream sauce, then lifted it to Victoria's lush lips. She purred as she chewed, her nails raking along his thigh as she swallowed. Pride and pleasure slid through him along with the heat from two fingers of fine Scotch.

She shook her head when he speared another slice. "No more. I can't eat another bite."

Setting the fork down, he leaned closer and licked a spot of cream from the corner of her mouth. He'd never thought he would have a Familiar. Never believed he'd want the responsibility. But looking after Victoria—feeding her, bathing her, loving her—was the reason he breathed.

"You brought a movie home," he reminded. "Do you want to watch it?"

"Do you?" Her voice was soft and husky, her cheeks flushed with vitality.

She'd been too thin when they first met, suffering from the lack of a master to care for her. She had lost her previous warlock, Darius, two centuries before, and neglect had taken its toll on both her appearance and her temperament. She'd been near feral, taunting the High Council with random acts of mischief and outwitting the numerous Hunters they sent to tame her.

Loving that spirit in her, Max had been careful in his care of her since she'd become his, maintaining the firm hand Familiars thrived under, yet giving her enough room to continue to challenge him. It was a delicate balance, one that kept them both content. He loved her with every breath in his body, desired her with a depth of need that was unquenchable.

"Let's watch it," he said, wanting to hold her while he considered their next best steps. He'd gotten more than an orgasm earlier; he had gained an understanding of just how dangerous his hunt for Sirius and Xander was. The magic he'd poured into Victoria had been tainted and she had cleansed it for him, restoring his equanimity, but at what cost to herself?

Victoria carried the wine and goblets into the living room while he cleared the table. When he joined her in the vast space of their loft's living room, he found candles flickering on every surface and his woman curled on the couch with the remote in her hand. He took a moment to study her body, gilded by candlelight, then lit the fireplace with a snap of his fingers. Sinking onto the couch, he smiled as she snuggled against him and started the movie. Her selection of *The Expendables 2* had him grinning. It was just so . . . *her*. Reclining into the cushions, he stroked his fingers through her hair and thought of the most efficient way to lure his prey out into the open.

The movie was halfway over when he decided Victoria was due a reward. He knew submission didn't come easy to her, partly because of her nature and partly because of Darius, who had gifted her with his magic as he lay dying from a battle with the Triumvirate. She was the most powerful Familiar the Council had ever heard of, and her pairing with him, the most accomplished Hunter, made her even more powerful. Ceding control was difficult for her, which made her doing so extremely precious to him.

Grateful for her love and trust, he stroked his hand down the graceful curve of her spine, then slipped beneath the hem of her robe to play with her.

She turned her head to nuzzle into him, her breath hot against his throat as she whispered, "Oh, Max . . . I love it when you touch me."

He pulled her onto his lap facing the television, splaying her legs on either side of his to open her to his questing touch. Her head lolled on his shoulder, her breath quickening as he parted her and massaged her clit. Turning his head, he rimmed the shell of her ear with his tongue, his cock hard and aching against the curve of her ass.

"I love touching you," he said softly, sliding one finger into her plush, silky cunt.

She lowered the surround-sound volume with her power, her hand covering the one he slid between the halves of her robe to cup her breast. "You need me, Max. Not just in your life and your bed, but in your work. Especially with a hunt like this."

He withdrew his slickened finger and returned with two, thrusting gently into her trembling cleft. "They'll gun for you in order to get to me."

"Of course they will." She sucked in a shaky breath as he deliberately coaxed her to a fever pitch, his fingertips massaging the sensitive tissues inside her. "But we're stronger together than apart."

Licking into her ear, he pressed the heel of his palm into her clit. She gasped and climaxed, rippling around him. The feel of her writhing in his lap was delicious. He wondered how he'd survived before he found her. When he contemplated his past, it seemed no more than shadows, memories that lacked clarity and definition. Worlds away from the vibrancy of his current existence.

The rest of the movie passed in a blur, his attention solely on the treasure in his arms. He slid his fingers in and out of her in a deliberately leisurely way, fucking her gently, making her come repeatedly until she begged for his cock.

When the credits began to roll, he cupped her jaw and turned her head. He took her mouth with all the hunger surging inside him, the need for her that was never fully appeased. She whimpered as the kiss grew reckless and greedy, his tongue thrusting deep and fast, lapping up the intoxicating taste of her.

Victoria twisted in his arms, facing and straddling him, her hands pushing into his hair. His breath soughed from his lungs; his cock was wet with anticipation.

"Time to play, kitten," he said gruffly.

Victoria pulled back to meet Max's heavy-lidded gaze. "I need more than this. I need you to need me, Max. For everything. Especially your work."

Shadows passed through his eyes. The air around them

grew charged, became heavy and electrified. Power pulsed off him in waves, lapping against her senses like waves on a beach.

His lips thinned into a grim line. "I'm not liking how you're bringing this discussion into playtime. You can't lead me around by my dick, Victoria. But you can damn well piss me off by trying."

She felt the sash of her robe slither around her wrists, binding them together behind her. Her breathing quickened until her chest was lifting and falling rapidly. Her pussy grew slick with wanting, her body preparing for the delicious invasion of his. When his hands gripped her hips, she shivered, her desire sharpened by the fine edge of fear. She knew he'd die before he ever hurt her, but his was a dark soul, his sexual hungers ferocious and insatiable, his need to dominate her an intrinsic part of their love affair.

In the time they'd been together, he'd taken her body in ways she could never have imagined, pushed her to her limits and beyond. He was a skilled lover, master of her desires and his own, his control unwavering.

With effortless strength, he lifted and positioned her, holding her aloft above the broad head of his cock. It notched into the clenching opening of her sex, then pushed in the few inches required for her knees to sink into the sofa cushions. She gasped at the teasing fullness, the taunting pressure spurring the anticipation of feeling his thick length sliding deep.

"Don't move," he warned darkly, forbidding her from sinking into his lap. "You'll take my cock when I give it to you."

Running his hand tenderly up her spine, Max cupped her nape and urged her to bend forward so he could take her mouth. Her eyes closed as their lips touched and the angle of his penetration pressed hard against her G-spot. She clenched around the plush head, hungry for the feel of it tunneling deeper and stretching her.

"Max," she whimpered, desperate for friction.

"Milk my dick, kitten. Show me how much you want it."

Victoria tightened down, rippling greedily, her aching sex trying to pull him inside her.

With a rough tug on her hips, Max obliged her, yanking her onto his raging erection with a force that drove a cry from her.

"*Max!*"

He groaned. His gorgeous face was flushed and taut, lines carved by the ecstasy of their joining. He ground his hips upward, screwing deep. "Hot, tight little fuck."

With her wrists bound at her lower back and her canted position, she had no leverage. She could only give her weight over to Max and let him use her as he needed, let him hold her in place while he thrust into her.

The act of giving herself so completely to him, of surrendering her body without reservation, was profoundly arousing. She grew wetter by the moment, her pussy quivering along his plunging length in helpless delight. Erotic sounds filled the room—Max's growls and her deep purrs, the slap of flesh meeting flesh, and the soft sucking of her creamy sex as he shafted her.

"Fuck me," he ordered, his hands straightening her angle so that she was upright. Catching her nipples between his thumb and forefinger, he rolled and tugged as she rode his cock. The wicked pulling on her sensitive flesh echoed between her legs. He pinched her hard enough to make her cry out, then cupped her breasts in his palms, kneading them to soothe the sting. All the while her hips pounded into his, his cock bottoming out on every deep thrust.

His breath gusted across her skin as he whispered darkly, "You feel so good. So wet and tight. Your cunt is squeezing me like a fist. I'm seconds away from coming hard in you."

"Yes," she gasped, her sex spasming in expectation, sucking him greedily.

His arms banded like steel around her. With a feral growl, he climaxed, spurting with such violence she felt it. His magic hit her like a sledgehammer, invading in a deluge, the taint of black magic wrenching a scream from her throat.

Her Familiar power enhanced Max's magic and cycled it back into him. He seized as it hit him, his breath hissing as his climax was spurred by the power rush, his cock swelling as he pumped her full of hot creamy semen.

Victoria trembled with the need to come, her pussy primed and so ready. But he hadn't told her she could and her body hovered in anticipation of the command.

Pushing to his feet, Max turned and bore her to the couch, looming over her with his big, powerful body. His hips lunged, plunging his thick cock deep inside her. He fucked her roughly, his control barely maintained, his demand for her climax implicit in the way he took her. Gripping the sofa arm, he powered into her, driving her to orgasm with long, fluid thrusts.

"Come," he growled. "Come now."

Victoria's back bowed as the pleasure speared through her, her sex tightening, then convulsing around him. She cried out, trembling, racked with love and longing and a desperate surge of magic. Power exploded from her, snuffing out the candles, then reigniting them with bright licks of flame. Max arched upward, his head thrown back with a virile snarl. He became the eye of the storm, his body the nexus of the magical tempest.

She clung to him as it ravaged him, the anchor he needed yet refused to reach for.

Four

$\mathcal{I}$n the early hours of the morning, Max slipped from bed, careful not to wake Victoria, who slept deeply. She might not realize it yet, but he was draining her, his magic greedily tapping into hers. Such was the way of parasitic black magic. It was ravenous and soul destroying, turning warlocks and witches into junkies who cared for nothing as much as they did their next fix.

He pulled on his pants and tied the drawstring as he moved out into the living room. Over the next hour, he increased the wards around the loft, tightening security to protect his most valuable possession. He'd nearly lost Victoria in the battle against the Triumvirate and had nearly lost his mind in the process. He had crossed a line that night, using both white and black magic to lure her back from the Transcendual Realm. He'd changed then, been stained by that violation of a sacred law. The Council chose not to disavow him, because he was too valuable to Them as a warlock who would do whatever was necessary.

Once he'd secured their home, he moved into the bedroom. The woman who slept in his bed was stretched out like a cat, her arms above her head and her legs extended. Soft purrs rumbled in the air, filling him with a contentment he'd never known before her. The deep purple satin sheet was draped over her pale skin, covering her taut belly but leaving one breast and leg exposed.

He shouldn't have come home to her after starting the hunt. He should've stayed away until it was over.

"Max."

Managing a smile, he leaned over and pressed a kiss to Victoria's sleep-soft mouth. "Good morning."

"Why are you out of bed?"

He nuzzled his nose against hers, then straightened. "Planning what to feed you for breakfast."

"Umm . . ." She smiled her catlike smile, a provocation his body responded to instantly.

"Would you like to shower before or after?" He enjoyed Victoria any way he could get her, but naked and wet was one of his favorites.

"I want to lie in bed with you all day."

Max took a deep breath, wanting the same thing but knowing he couldn't afford to lose an entire day. As long as Powell and Barnes were out there, Victoria was at risk. "Soon, kitten."

Her gaze narrowed. "You're starting the hunt?"

"No time like the present." He headed to the kitchen, hoping to avoid a fight.

It was a fruitless exercise, he realized, when a sleek black cat raced by him and promptly sat on the threshold to the kitchen. Victoria couldn't keep up with his long stride in her human form, but she had him beat in her feline one.

"Sweetheart," he said sternly, moving to step over her and getting swiped at instead.

She shifted, appearing before him in all her naked glory.

His breath caught as it always did when he saw her bared. He'd never wanted any woman more.

With an impatient wave of his fingers, he covered her in a red silk robe, loving the way the color contrasted with her creamy skin and dark hair. "We're not rehashing this."

"At least tell me where you're going and how long you'll be gone."

His brows rose. "That sounded like an order."

"Maybe it was. You came after me, Max, when I tried to walk out of your life. You claimed me. If you didn't want the hassle, you should've let the Council pair me with Gabriel, as They intended—"

Victoria! Magic surged out of him along with acidic jealousy. He couldn't think of her with someone else, it made him furious. "You're pushing me, kitten."

"You're pushing me aside!" she argued.

Recognizing the fear in her eyes, Max pulled her close and pressed his lips to her forehead. "They're close," he said softly. "Too close. I need to know you're safe or I'll give them an opening that wouldn't be there otherwise."

"I feel them, too," she said, snuggling into him. "You're strong, Max. The strongest warlock I've ever come across, but it's two against one! At least with me, you can even the odds."

"I can even the odds without risking you."

"With black magic. That's too dangerous!"

He rested his chin on the top of her head. "Like calls to like. I have to draw them in."

"Which is why it's even more important that I be with you!" Pulling back, she looked up at him, her emerald eyes pleading. "I can keep you grounded."

"Or I could taint Darius's magic and push you too far."

"Is that what you're afraid of?"

Releasing her, Max ran a hand through his hair. "Among other things."

Her eyes widened, then softened with love. "You've never been afraid before."

"I never had anything to lose."

She cupped his cheek and lifted to her tiptoes to press her mouth to his. Her tongue darted over his lips, leaving the taste of her behind.

"Don't worry about me," she murmured.

"I can't stop it." He caught her waist, felt how fragile she was. For all her power, she was soft and delicate. "I won't make it without you, Victoria. You're everything to me."

"Max . . ."

He kissed her, silencing the pleas that strove to weaken his resolve.

Victoria worked hard to accept Max's decision, fighting the sense of foreboding that had her agitated. The last thing she wanted was to distract Max in any way from his hunt, despite her certainty that he shouldn't go alone.

He slid the zipper up the back of her skirt, then ran his hands over her hips. His lips touched her nape and her eyes closed. She'd become so accustomed to being cared for, she had been lost the two days Max had been gone.

"Ready?" he asked.

She nodded, though it was a lie. He would take her to work, then disappear, and she had no idea when—or if—he'd be back. It wasn't in her nature to accept not getting her way. Max was the only one who ever told her no. She'd learned to accept it, knowing the reward would be worth suffering the denial, but she couldn't see a reward here, beyond hoping and praying that he returned to her alive and untainted.

His hand linked with hers, and in the blink of an eye, they were around the corner from the St. John. She was struck once again by the breadth of his power . . . and turned on by it. Max wielded his magic so easily. Effortlessly. And carried the weight of it with an air of command that was sexy and devastatingly attractive.

"Keep your guard up," he said quietly.

"Yes, of course."

He kissed her forehead, her eyelids, the tip of her nose, then finally her mouth. He smelled wonderful and looked even better. Tall and powerfully lean, his broad shoulders hugged by tailored Armani. The black three-piece suit complemented his dark hair, framing a sculpted face that still made her breath catch when he smiled.

"Stop worrying," he admonished.

Overwhelmed by fear for him, Victoria caught him by the tie. "Refuse the hunt. Don't go."

"Victoria—"

"They can send someone else."

"I don't want them to send someone else."

She froze. "Why? Did the High Council threaten you? Did They threaten *me*?"

"No." He cupped her nape in his hand and his silver gaze slid over her face. "Hunting is what I do, Victoria. You've always known that."

"Yes, but there will be other hunts. You don't have to take—"

"None this challenging."

She stared at him, her breath quick and her pulse racing. "You'd choose this hunt over me?"

"Don't." His face hardened. "I am who I am. You wouldn't want me any other way."

"I want you alive!"

"You want a predator, just like you. You ruined every Hunter that stalked you before I came along. Ruined them and tossed them aside." He caught her by the arms and lifted her onto her toes. "I hunt and I catch. I caught you. I've kept you. And I'll come home to you. Don't try to leash me, kitten. I won't have it and you wouldn't want it."

I love you.

She watched his eyes close as her words drifted through his mind. *I love you back.*

Max wrapped her up in his arms. He held her close and she didn't care that they were embracing on the street with people walking by. She didn't want to let go.

"Come on," he said finally, pulling back. "The sooner I get started, the sooner it'll be over."

"You already started."

His chest expanded on a deep, slow breath. A silent admission.

With his hand at her elbow, he led her around the corner

and came to an abrupt stop. Victoria stumbled into his side, gathering her power to face the threat. It wasn't what she expected.

She wasn't what Victoria expected.

Petite and voluptuous, the blonde waiting in front of the St. John was clearly expecting Max, as evidenced by the wide curve of her pink lips when she saw him. The tension that gripped Max's frame in response made Victoria's claws extend and a low growl rumble in her chest.

The woman was a witch. A powerful one. Victoria could feel the magic pulsing off her. Wearing towering stilettos and a sleeveless blue wrap dress that matched her eyes, the witch was being eyed appreciatively by every man within viewing distance.

"There you are," the blonde said, walking toward them in a leisurely, seductive way, her waist-length hair swaying gently. "You always like to keep me waiting. Not that I've ever had cause to complain in the end."

She ignored Victoria altogether.

"Jezebel," Max drawled. "What are you doing here?"

"Once I heard your name linked with Powell and Barnes, nothing could've kept me away. A dual hunt like this comes once in a lifetime." Her mouth curved and her blue eyes sparkled with feminine appreciation as they raked him from head to toe. "Considering how long we live, darling, that's saying something."

She stopped in front of Max and ran her hand down his tie, disregarding the fact that he was holding hands with another woman. He caught her by the wrist, which only made her smile widen.

"Jezebel, let me introduce you to Victoria. Sweetheart, this is Jezebel . . . an old friend."

Victoria bristled, aware of precisely how good a "friend" Jezebel had been to Max. The sensual awareness between them was obvious, as was their chemistry.

You fucked that? she asked.

Sheath the claws, kitten.

Jezebel flicked her gaze to Victoria for the first time. "A Familiar. How quaint. I'd heard you'd paired with one, but couldn't believe it."

"Believe it," Victoria growled, punctuating her words with a sudden gust of air that sent the blonde stumbling back a step to totter on her heels.

"Victoria," Max warned. *You can't take her on, she's too powerful.*

I don't care. She's talking around me as if I'm not here!

She's trying to get to you, he said grimly, *and you're letting her.*

Jezebel laughed huskily and shook out her hair. "She's not tamed at all, is she? Knowing you, Max, you find that a challenging form of entertainment."

Victoria waited for him to say something in her defense. Instead, Max said, "Let me see Victoria to the door, then we'll talk."

If you head off with that bitch, I'm going to be pissed.

You're already pissed, he retorted.

Max!

She felt a flare of magic that cut off their sharing of thoughts and her stomach knotted. He was changing. Worse, he was disconnecting from her in the process.

His perfunctory kiss on her forehead and briskly spoken

I love you did nothing to alleviate the fear that she was losing him.

Victoria watched through the revolving glass entrance doors of the St. John as Jezebel linked her arm with Max's and led him across the street. They made a striking couple—Max tall and dark, Jezebel petite and golden. There was also a natural familiarity in the way they moved together.

He'd been with her for a considerable length of time at some point.

Seething with jealousy and territorial possessiveness, Victoria turned on her heel and headed toward the elevators, determined to find out exactly how much of a threat Jezebel was.

Five

"Too easy," Xander said, his eyes on the stiff-backed Familiar as she marched through the entrance of the St. John Hotel. An entrance he'd empowered with a spell that provoked restlessness.

Sirius's head turned as he followed Westin crossing the street. He had more than a score to settle. He wanted to hit the High Council where it hurt, and turning their golden boy into a dark master would be a crippling blow. Westin had already done much of the work for them by breaching the Transcendual Realm. His aura was tainted by the effort. He should be rogue . . . hunted . . . But Westin always got away with everything. The Council was more afraid of losing him than keeping him.

"We'll need more than that little run-in," Sirius murmured. "We've got one shot at tainting that Familiar. If we fuck it up, Westin will know and take steps. We won't get a second chance."

"Got something in mind?"

"He needs to have a reason not to send Patridge off on her merry way. He'll keep her close if he thinks she's a target."

"You want to take 'em both on at once?" Xander turned wide eyes to Sirius. "Now we're talking!"

Sirius transferred to a point ahead of Westin and his hot piece of ass, lingering in half form in the shadows. Extending a ghostly hand—the shape formed by grasping tendrils of gray smoke—Sirius cast a spell that formed a dark puddle on the sidewalk. It writhed gently, ripples forming as it sensed its prey approaching. Xander joined him just as Jezebel Patridge stepped into the deceptively shallow-looking water.

She screamed as the water rushed up her body like a sleeve, greedily hugging the curves that Westin was intimately familiar with. A laugh bubbled up in Sirius's throat—

Westin pivoted abruptly. Thrusting out both hands, he launched a ball of energy from his fingertips. It struck Sirius in the chest with unerring precision. It sent him spinning deeper into the shadows. Then farther, into oblivion.

Arianna settled into the seat in front of Victoria's desk and crossed her jeans-clad legs. The witch wore her red hair cropped short and spiked. Brown eyes rimmed heavily with liner and burgundy-stained lips emphasized the paleness of her flawless skin. It also caused people to misjudge her as delinquent and ungifted.

Fact was, Arianna was the best scribing witch Victoria had

ever come across. Whether it was information or an object, Arianna could find it.

"Westin's been shagging Jezebel Patridge on and off for the last twenty years or so," the witch announced, sliding into her customary slouch.

Victoria caught her breath, then exhaled in a rush. "Twenty *years?*"

"Nothing serious, from what I heard. Most of those I talked to describe it as a friends-with-benefits kind of thing. He certainly hasn't been monogamous. He's been bed-hopping the whole time. Although beds aren't always involved, I've been told."

That didn't make Victoria feel better. "Twenty years is a long time."

"Yeah." Arianna shrugged. "There are no gruesome stories about a nasty breakup or anything. I get the impression it's more like a breather between the two rather than a split."

Pushing back from her desk, Victoria stood and began to pace. Her feline need to roam when feeling caged had kicked in with a vengeance. Everything seemed off. The hotel staff was being run ragged by guest queries and requests. She wondered if the restlessness she felt was affecting everyone around her or if the reverse was true.

"Also," Arianna went on, "Patridge has become somewhat of an expert on Westin and his technique. She's given lectures at the academy breaking down the methods he used to capture Barnes and Powell, so the information I gathered was mostly authored by her."

Which meant Jezebel might actually be useful to Max on a

hunt for those same rogues, not that Victoria was soothed by the thought. She'd researched Max when they first met, but only superficially. She realized that she had subconsciously—but likely deliberately—avoided digging into his personal life. Even then she couldn't bear the thought of him with someone else.

"Have they hunted together in the past?" Victoria asked, pausing at the window to stare out at the urban jungle spread before her. Fog hung over the city, obscuring the upper halves of the skyscrapers that dotted the landscape for miles. Below, traffic slid along the streets in endless ribbons, the cacophony of the city lapping at her heightened feline senses.

"Not that I could find. Listen, don't get twisted out of shape over this. No guy is worth it. Besides, the binding works both ways. You hardly ever hear about mated pairs fucking around on each other."

"You hardly ever hear about mated pairs composed of a Hunter and Familiar either," Victoria said drily, turning to face the redhead again.

"True." Arianna stood and withdrew a flash drive from her pocket. She tossed it to Victoria. "But he's not worth shit if he can't keep it in his pants for you."

Victoria caught the drive and her hand closed like a fist around it. The level of Max's experience had been evident from the moment she laid eyes on him. Every inch of him exuded sin and sex. From the sensual way he moved to the confidence in his eyes. And when he touched her, his skill blew her mind.

Max Westin fucked like a god.

Still, men who played sometimes strayed, and clearly Jezebel had something Max hadn't minded tapping over and over again. For *decades*.

"I'll bill you," Arianna said, heading out.

Gathering her resolve, Victoria sat at her desk and plugged in the flash drive. She was sliding the arrow over to click the drive open when she felt the first tingles of Max's magic tapping into hers. Without further warning, the force of the draw exploded. It sucked at her strength like a raging vortex, dragging her down until she tumbled from the chair to the floor.

"Damn it." Jezebel stared into the steaming mug of tea she held with both hands. "That attack shouldn't have scared me as much as it did."

Max stood over her, his thoughts grim.

She tilted her head back to look up at him. She wore one of his robes, her clothes discarded because of the taint that clung to them. She'd showered, but her hair and makeup were flawless as usual, reapplied with a simple spell.

He glanced at the clock, knowing Victoria would be leaving the hotel within the hour. He couldn't risk her coming home alone and unprotected, no matter how much power she carried on her own. "I have to go."

"Don't go after them without me!" Jezebel protested, pushing to her feet, a move that caused the robe she was wearing to part and reveal the length of her bare leg.

Once, the sight would've stirred his lust and hardened his cock, but it had little effect on him now. His thoughts were with Victoria.

They weren't all focused on keeping her safe.

Spurred by the rush of wielding the full force of his magic, his desire was white-hot, his mind racing through one erotic scenario after another. He wanted his woman stripped and bound, her lithe body spread and open to his lust. Only then would she be open to the rush of magic that would replenish what he'd taken from her earlier. Replenish him as well, building the reserves he'd need to vanquish his prey once and for all.

"I'm going to get Victoria," he said, his voice hoarse from the depth of his need.

Jezebel's mouth tightened at the mention of his Familiar. "I'll go with you."

"Not a good idea." His kitten already had her fur ruffled over Jezebel. But more relevant was the fact that when he got his hands on Victoria, he wasn't letting go until he'd come his last drop in her. It was certain Jezebel wouldn't appreciate cooling her heels while he did so.

"Doesn't she know what you're like, Max?" she asked, her eyes diamond bright . . . and equally hard. "Jealousy is pointless when it comes to you."

"I'm not the man who used to fuck you, Jezebel."

"Has she tamed you, then?" she goaded softly. "What a shame."

His mouth quirked and he stepped away, deciding not to bother with his vest and jacket. His blood was hot with the hunt, making him want bare skin over clothing. "You and I can be friends, Jezebel, or not. That's up to you."

She materialized naked and on her knees in front of him, her head bowed in a pose of submission she knew would goad his dominant nature. Her hands rested on her knees, her body waiting for his command. "As long as I get your cock inside me, you can call me whatever you want. I need it, Max. I feel empty without it."

Max took a deep breath. His body was hard and aching, and black magic still clung faintly to Jezebel, calling to the darkness inside him. His mind retained heated memories of his past with Jezebel, a true submissive, which prompted a reluctant response to the sight of her capitulation. While Victoria eventually surrendered, it wasn't without some resistance. She gave him control because she chose to please him, not because she had a true compulsion to do so.

But she was the only woman he wanted. The only one who could soothe the beast inside him.

He flashed to Victoria's office, incited by the thought of subduing her naturally defiant nature. In that respect Jezebel was right—he loved the challenge.

His kitten sat behind her desk, a frown of concentration on her beautiful face as she read from her monitor. Her long slender legs were crossed at the ankles beneath her desk, while diamond studs sparkled with multihued fire at her ears. He flashed behind her, reading over her shoulder, intrigued by the realization that she was studying up on him.

Gods, he loved her. Loved that she was as consumed by him as he was by her.

"I want your cunt," he said gruffly, driven hard by his need. "And your ass."

Her head swiveled toward him and she pushed to her feet. "Max. What the fuck happened today?"

He snapped his fingers and removed her clothes, leaving her as naked as Jezebel had been. The two women could not have been more different, not just in their appearance but also in their effect on him. While his lust had been stirred instinctually by Jezebel, what Victoria incited in him was a different sort of hunger altogether. Ravenous. Insatiable. Soul-deep. One goaded as much by his love for her as it was by his desire for her body.

"On your knees," he ordered.

"Max—"

"*Now.*"

Her jaw tightened before she shoved her chair aside and obeyed. That hint of rebellion pushed him further. He touched her shoulder and took her across town to his loft, a space he no longer resided in but kept as a playroom.

"That's right, kitten. It's time to play."

Six

Victoria stiffened when she realized where Max had taken her. Unlike the apartment he shared with her now, with its warm palette of honey-hued hardwood floors and cream-colored walls, Max's former bachelor pad was industrial in style. An acid-washed cement floor chilled her bare knees, while exposed ductwork hovered above her head and pale gray walls surrounded them along with an impressive collection of sexual paraphernalia.

Her pussy clenched with longing, her body trained to anticipate the pleasures to be found in the familiar space. But anger and jealousy simmered inside her. She didn't want to play. She wanted to fight.

"Where's Jezebel?" she asked, keeping her head defiantly back to stare up at him.

His mouth curved in a slow, sexy smile. "Your possessiveness makes my dick so hard it hurts."

"Are you sure your hard-on isn't due to seeing the woman you've been banging for twenty years!"

Max began to undress, freeing the buttons of his shirt one by one, exposing the hard expanse of his chest one inch at a time. "I could be in her now," he drawled, his gaze heavy-lidded with the arousal that strained against the zipper of his slacks. "She's naked in our apartment. On her knees and desperate for my cock."

She gasped, then moved to rise. "What the fuck?"

With a careless wave of his hand, he undressed her and sent her across the room to the bed. A bondage bar appeared on the red satin beside her and a tremor ran through her at the sight of it. Soon she'd be helpless and exposed, her body restrained and arranged to service him. Before Max, she had never imagined that she would crave that level of vulnerability and loss of control. Now she couldn't imagine doing without it. He told her what to do, what to feel. And in return she'd orgasm until she was insensate with pleasure.

"You can't hold my past against me," he said, his voice tight and low. "I like to fuck. So do you. For the rest of our lives, we'll be fucking only each other. Nothing else matters."

He approached her with that wickedly sexy stride, one that promised as much as she could take, his body rippling with muscle. His erection was thick and long, the wide head glistening with his excitement. It curved up to his navel, the size of him enough to make her thighs squeeze together against the ache he created. She pushed up and curled her legs beneath her, wanting him but wanting answers, too.

It was harder to stay focused on talking than she cared to admit. She knew exactly how that big dick felt inside her, how it stretched her and rubbed all the most sensitive spots, how she writhed beneath his hard body and begged for him to give it all to her.

"Max . . ."

"I should be hunting."

He reached the end of the bed and she saw the sweat glistening on the steely ridges of his abdomen. A creamy, glistening drop of pre-cum slid lovingly down the thickly veined length of his cock.

He was so *hot for it.*

"Instead," he went on, "I can't breathe for wanting you. Can't think. Can't wait to sink my dick inside you and come until my balls stop aching."

"Did she make you this hot?" Victoria asked softly.

"Never." He grabbed the bar in his fist, the bright chrome suddenly looking dangerous when held by that beautifully defined arm. "I've never felt this way about anyone. You know that. Stop doubting me, Victoria. It's starting to piss me off."

She took a quick breath, her nipples hard and aching. He stood there waiting, a formidable male in full rut, his face harsh in its unyielding masculine beauty. His virile body strained with the need to mount her.

"You know what to do," he said huskily. "Don't make me wait."

Victoria turned and stretched out facedown, spreading her legs to accommodate the bar. Her pulse quickened, spurring her breathing and her desire. Still, she couldn't hold back from saying, "She wants you back."

His former lover had been in their home, naked and willing. What excuse could there be for that?

"I don't care what she wants. I only care about you." Butter-soft leather wrapped around her ankle and tightened. "Your magic is in me. I feel you. Smell you." His hand slid adoringly up the back of her leg. "Taste you."

She moaned. "Why is she in our home?"

"Why are you obsessed with her?" His hand came down hard on her buttock, the sound of flesh hitting flesh cracking like thunder. She cried out and squirmed, her skin on fire from the spanking. "You know I love you too much. There's no room for anyone else."

His voice throbbed with emotion and Victoria's eyes closed tightly. His hand smacked hard against her other cheek and the heat swept through her legs, swelling the lips of her sex.

"You don't know how you look together," she moaned. "How obvious it is that you enjoy fucking each other. You wouldn't understand unless you saw me with one of the Hunters that came before you. See how they look at me in a way that says they know what it feels like to have me suck them off . . . how it feels inside me . . ."

"*Victoria,*" he growled, just before he bent and sank his teeth into her hip. Punishing her. Marking her.

She sobbed, so aroused her body hurt. "I hate that she knows how good you feel. The sounds you make. I hate that you wanted her so much."

"Not as much as I want you," he breathed, nuzzling his cheek against hers. "Not even close."

The other leather cuff magically secured itself on her ankle.

"She was targeted today," he told her roughly. "Struck right on the street in broad daylight with me beside her."

Victoria's breath caught.

"I told you how dangerous this hunt is. Told you they'd come after those around me. It could've been you—"

His voice broke. Sliding his hands gently beneath her torso, he cupped her breasts and pulled her up onto her knees. He moved onto the bed, tugging and milking her nipples. His chest was hot and hard at her shoulder, his hair a soft caress against her neck. Her back arched, pressing her aching breasts into his hands, her balance fully dependent upon his strength.

"It could have been you," he said again, his lips at her throat. "And I couldn't have borne it, Victoria."

"Let me help you. Please."

"You'll help me now." He gripped her nape firmly in his hand and urged her forward, anchoring her by the waist as she folded to press her cheek against the bed.

Her arms pushed through her splayed legs and were instantly bound to the bar by leather cuffs. She was helpless and unable to move, her hips arched high and held wide, her sex open and positioned for his pleasure. The deepest penetration.

Victoria creamed with excitement and anticipation. The more restrained she was, the hotter Max got. The hotter he got, the more she wanted him.

He straightened and snapped his fingers. It was the only warning she got before the lash of a flogger stung the back of her thighs. She moaned into the comforter, absorbing the sting of pain into her clenching core. Inside her, something rebelled. But it wasn't stronger than her desire. Max took her places she didn't want to go and yet couldn't wait to get to.

His hand stroked over the heated, smarting skin. "Stop fighting me."

"Fuck me."

The flogger came down again. She gritted her teeth against the pleasure/pain. Max used the perfect amount of force, his actions skilled and methodical. She couldn't help but wonder at the practice he'd had, the darkness in him that made him need unequivocal subjugation.

"Stop analyzing me." His voice was low and controlled, quietly authoritative. He whipped her again, striking new flesh with unerring precision. When he was done, the temporary marks he left would form a clear artistic pattern. "Stop doubting me."

"Max . . ." The plea in her voice came from a wellspring inside her that only he'd ever tapped.

"Stop second-guessing me. I spent only two days away, Victoria, and you seem to have forgotten what you promised me." The suede straps whacked against her buttocks. "To serve, obey, and please me. To never question an order or deny me anything. To never tell me no."

"I give you more than I've ever given anyone."

The flogger came down harder. Not enough to bruise her, but enough to tighten her attention on him. On the sound of his steady, unaffected breathing. On her pounding heartbeat.

To make her wetter. Needier.

"You're too focused on your vulnerability," he crooned, massaging her burning flesh with gentle fingertips. "It was a gift you promised me when I claimed you, but you've never really given it, have you? But I've kept my promise to you. To cherish you . . . treasure you . . . to keep you safe."

"Your life is dangerous, Max. *You're* dangerous. That's part of the package."

"Are you still arguing with me, kitten?"

She tensed, but he switched his game on her. From pain to pleasure. His clever fingers gliding over her exposed pussy. She shivered as sensation darted through her, tightening her skin. A gasp escaped her as he rubbed her clit, circling over it with featherlight pressure.

"Such a pretty cunt," he murmured, his breath hot against her glistening folds. His tongue teased her, rimming the opening to her sex. "Soft and tight and creamy. I'm going to fuck it hard and have the most delicious orgasm inside it. I'm going to pump you full of thick, slick cum."

"Yes. Max . . . please."

He straightened and caught her hips, rolling her carefully to her back. She lay splayed before him, her ankles and wrists by her ears. "You won't come."

She whimpered and swallowed hard. "I've obeyed you."

His silvery eyes stared down at her from within a face sharpened by lust. There was a wildness in his gaze she hadn't caught before. "In practice, if not in spirit?"

Alarm tingled through her. "What happened today, Max?"

Gripping the back of her thigh, he took his cock in hand and stroked it between the lips of her sex, coating her with the pre-cum that leaked copiously from the tip. He was so big and hard, thicker than she'd seen before. Veins coursed down the length of the shaft as well as up his straining forearms, his body poised to mate as hard as he'd promised.

"I vanquished one of them," he bit out between clenched teeth.

Then he rammed his cock into her, his magic slamming into her with equal force.

Victoria's mouth opened on a silent scream. Possessed by him. Ravaged.

Seven

She came. She couldn't stop it. Primed and too ready as she was, it took only the brutal thrust of that big cock into her tender sex to set her off. Dark magic pounded at her as hard as Max did, every plunge into her pussy accompanied by a surge of power. She quaked beneath him, her sex milking his shuttling cock, her vision blackening for a moment as her blood coursed hot and fast.

Gripping the backs of her thighs, he kept her pinned and spread for his maddened fucking, a captured vessel for his raging lust. His hips powered between hers, his sac smacking rhythmically against the curves of her ass. His cock pumped her slick pussy, plunging in and out, his body working like a well-oiled and high-performance machine.

"Mine," he growled. "Mine."

"Max . . . please." Victoria didn't know if she was begging him to stop or never to stop, her body reveling in the rough treatment, loving the act of being used for the sole purpose of giving him pleasure. His cock drove relentlessly into her, thrusting through grasping and greedy tissue, sliding furiously across sensitized flesh.

He threw his dark head back, his hair drifting around his broad shoulders, muscles straining and neck arching as a rush of white-hot semen spurted inside her. Her hands and feet flexed with the need for movement, her chest heaving for breath as he emptied himself without missing a stroke. A virile snarl reverberated through the massive room, a sound of primitive masculine satisfaction that had her coming again.

Her body was still racked by the potent climax when he yanked free of her. The bar disappeared and he flipped her, mounting her from behind and hammering deep. Sprawled prone on the bed and blanketed by his fevered, sweat-slick body, Victoria clawed at the comforter and bit into it, stifling the cries of pleasure she couldn't contain.

Her eyes rolled and then closed, her senses overloaded by the smell of Max's hardworking body, the feel of his muscles flexing against her as he succumbed to animal instinct and lost everything except the need to ride her and come in her. His cock retained its desperate hardness, his magic pulsed in her, flooding her. His aura was smoky and dark, tainted by magic he'd absorbed from the vanquishing earlier that day. She understood his black mood then. Understood what was driving him so hard.

She surrendered, opening herself in every way. Max felt it and snarled, his hands gripping hers, their fingers lacing tightly. Magic cycled between them, the essence cleansed as it filtered through them both.

His face pressed into the crook of her neck, his sweat blending with her own, his chest heaving with exertion. He fucked her like a man possessed, and maybe, in a way, he was. She could only take it, take him, and come. Over and over again.

I love you. He nudged her thigh wider with his knee so he could thrust deeper. *Love you.*

Victoria pressed her cheek to his. *I know.*

Xander straightened from his lounging pose in a darkened shop doorway across the street from the apartment building where Westin lived with St. John. The warlock had left earlier, a fact made evident by the sudden void where magic had pulsed before. Still, a quick reconnaissance had revealed he'd left powerful wards in place. That was to be expected.

What Xander hadn't anticipated was Westin's absorption of some of Sirius's magic. That development infuriated him. He'd carefully manipulated Sirius into thinking he was the bright one, giving him false confidence. Xander had planned every word and action to goad the other warlock into striking at Westin first. He'd deliberately appeared in the shadows at the precise moment of Sirius's attack, catching Westin's attention and thereby luring the Hunter to strike out and vanquish his foe. The plan had been for *him*, Xander, to absorb Sirius's power, not Westin. Then he would've been powerful enough to draw the attention of the Source of All Evil. He might have become as potent as the Triumvirate had once been.

But all wasn't lost. Westin would pour some of that hijacked magic into St. John, making it easier for Xander to do so as well. The Familiar had been feral once. A hefty dose of black magic and a tiny seed of doubt about Westin would push her over that edge again. Sirius had been useful in coming up with that plan. If Xander could turn St. John, she'd be uncontrollable, wild, and Westin would lose the augmentation she gave him. He'd also be knocked off his game by being at odds with his lover, and that's all Xander needed—a single opening.

"There you are," he murmured to himself as a lovely blonde spun through the revolving doors of the apartment building as if he'd conjured her.

Dressed in a new outfit composed of slim black slacks and a blue sleeveless blouse, Jezebel Patridge ignored the greeting of the doorman and glared at the world around her. She could've bridged the distance between the building and anywhere she chose to go, but she clearly had no idea where to end up and probably lacked the desire to leave. She wanted Westin. Taking off wasn't going to help her cause. But waiting around for him was clearly not sitting well.

Xander stepped out of shadows and sent out a soft pulse of magic to attract her attention. When she glanced his way, he shifted as if hiding from her gaze and set off at a brisk walk. Fleeing. Or so she'd think.

And she would chase him. She was a Hunter, after all. And he was a rogue, presently on the Council's most-wanted list.

Five minutes later, Patridge's hair was spread out in a golden halo on the dank ground of an alley, her chest split by a dual hit of magic.

Xander squeezed his wrist and smiled as he dripped his tainted blood into the cavity.

Max circled Victoria's nipple with his tongue, his hips rolling softly as he stirred his cock in her cum-soaked depths.

She mewled, her fingers stroking weakly along his back. She was exhausted, her short cap of hair wet with sweat, her skin flushed a rosy pink, her dark lashes fluttering over closed eyes.

He gentled her while soothing himself. He was as exhausted as she was by his violent need to dominate her. To rut in her until he doubted he could stand. And she'd let him.

It angered him that he hadn't seen his need for what it was—the black magic inside him seeking an outlet in his beloved Familiar. His soul mate. The woman he loved more than he'd ever thought himself capable of loving anyone.

Now her skin tasted of that taint, her addicting vanilla essence muskier and more provocative to his senses. He was spiraling down the drain and taking her with him.

Turning his head, he teased her other nipple with light laps of his tongue. "Am I hurting you?" he asked, his voice hoarse from the many times he'd roared his pleasure while coming.

"No," she whispered, her fingers digging into his ass with the barest force. "Don't stop."

His cock slid in and out of her leisurely, concern for her comfort foremost in his mind. He'd stop if he could, but he needed the connection, needed to be certain that everything was okay between them. The smell of her skin, the softness of her body, her touch . . . nothing in his life had ever been as necessary as she was.

Shifting carefully, he began to stroke the head of his cock over the sensitive bundle of nerves inside her. He felt the tension in her rise, listened for the catch in her breath. When she seized in orgasm, he groaned and followed her, coming along with the delicate rippling of her cunt.

He was gasping and shuddering with pleasure when he felt

the warding around his loft signal the presence of magickind. He was on his feet in an instant, his cock wet and semi-erect, his body tapping into his newly stored magical reserves to strengthen muscles weakened by hours of hard sex.

You have exceeded our expectations once again, the Council said, a multitude of voices speaking eerily as one—a hive mind of the most powerful witches and warlocks of all time. *You vanquished Sirius with astonishing swiftness.*

"That's what you wanted, isn't it?" he asked, tugging on a pair of jeans. He cast an eye toward the bed and saw that Victoria had curled onto her side in a catnap.

Your power is impressive. We would like to see a demonstration of it.

"The fact that Powell is dead is demonstration enough." He moved toward the front door, his right arm at his side, the palm filling with a ball of roiling magic.

Do not forget that it is because of our forbearance that you are not a hunted rogue now.

"Don't forget you'd still be chasing down Powell and likely losing Hunters if not for me. This is a symbiotic relationship, not a gift."

Let us see how long it takes for you to vanquish Barnes, They said snidely.

"Yeah," he agreed, reaching for the handle of his front door. "Let's see."

He wrenched it open and drew his arm back.

"Whoa!" Gabriel lifted both hands in surrender. "Kick back, killer."

Max's gaze narrowed, assessing the man he would always view as a rival. Gabriel Masters grinned, his hazel eyes lit with amusement. The dark-haired warlock was upper level, but not quite up to Max's skill. Still, he carried enough power to have been selected as Victoria's warlock . . . before Max had taken her as his own. "What are you doing here, Masters?"

They weren't friends, never had been. With both of them out on a hunt more often than not, they'd rarely had the chance to cross paths.

"Aren't you going to invite me in?" Masters asked.

Max stepped back and gestured the other man inside. Across the room, he conjured folding screens to hide the bed where his kitten slept. Still, the scent of her pheromones was heavy in the air, and Masters wasn't immune. The warlock shifted on his feet, his shoulders rolling back.

"Mine," Max warned in a low rumble.

"She's the reason I'm here." Masters faced him. "Word's spreading fast about the vanquishing today. Jezebel says you took Powell out with a single hit."

"So?"

"So everyone knows your Familiar helped you. I'm not the only Hunter thinking about taking on a Familiar now."

"It has its benefits," he conceded. "But Familiars are a helluva lot of work. If it were anyone but Victoria, I wouldn't think it'd be worth the effort."

"Yeah, I can smell how much work is involved." Masters's smile faded. "Some are asking if you're powerful enough now to challenge the High Council."

A chill ran down Max's spine. The Council wouldn't like that. They took all threats very, very seriously. If they viewed him as one, they'd take steps. And Victoria's augmentation was what gave him an advantage.

"I wouldn't go to the trouble if I could," he drawled, careful to hide his disquiet. "I've got everything I want right here."

"You do. Maybe others don't."

Max crossed his arms over his bare chest. "Don't bring revolution into my house."

Masters's lips curved wryly. "Why not? You brought it into magickind to begin with."

Eight

Victoria's stomach knotted at the news Gabriel Masters passed on to Max. She feigned sleep, as she rarely slept deeply while napping, and decided she wouldn't let on that she knew unless he told her directly.

She wondered if he'd anticipated this, if he'd kept her from hunting with him to avoid just this sort of thing. He wouldn't want to upset her, even if explaining kept them from fighting about his decision to exclude her.

Max showed Gabriel out and then padded over to the bed. She heard him, smelled him, felt soothed by his presence the closer he came to her. The bed dipped as he sat beside her. His hand stroked down her side.

"Kitten," he said quietly, bending toward her and pressing his lips to her shoulder. "I have to go."

When he straightened, she rolled to her back and looked up

at him. "Shouldn't you get some sleep? Or will you be home soon?"

"The sooner this hunt is over with, the better." His gray eyes softened as they looked down at her. "Then we'll go away for a while. Someplace tropical, maybe, where you'll be naked all day. Or snowbound, where I could spread you out in front of a fireplace."

She caught the hand he had resting on her hip and squeezed it. "Sounds wonderful."

"Do you want to stay here? Or should I take you back to the apartment?"

"Home." She sighed. "I have work to do. It was insane at the hotel today."

"Can you work from home the next few days?"

"Sure." She hated working away from the office, but she wasn't going to bitch. Max had enough on his mind.

"Let's get cleaned up, then," he murmured, a soft smile on his lips.

Thirty minutes later, Victoria felt a semblance of equanimity. Max had washed her from head to toe, his dexterous fingers kneading her scalp and every muscle. He was so good to her. So good for her.

He dressed her in a simple set of pajamas, choosing to secure each button himself rather than with magic. "There."

"Here." She lifted onto her tiptoes and kissed his jaw. "And I'll be waiting for you when you get back."

A rough sound escaped him and he pulled her close, wrapping his arms around her. He held her for a moment, then they were home. The abrupt introduction of sax music jolted her.

But the bigger shock came from the naked blonde in a leather collar who was strolling into the living room by way of the bedroom hallway.

"Max," Jezebel purred, stretching as if just waking. "I thought you were kidding about bringing your kitten home to play with us."

Victoria's gaze was riveted to the MAX engraved in the black leather circling the witch's neck and to the marks on her breasts that were perfectly laid out and aligned in Max's recognizable pattern.

"Jezebel," Max growled. "What the fuck do you think you're doing?"

"You, darling." She smiled and cupped her breasts, offering them up. "Any way you want."

Vicious magic surged within Victoria, thick and black and hot. It roiled and singed her hands, itching to be freed. "Bitch," she hissed, "you'd better vanish real quick."

"I told you, darling," Jezebel said, licking her lips as she tugged on her own nipples. "Familiars don't play well with others."

Max stalked toward her and Victoria lost it, unable to let him put his hands on another woman. Especially a naked woman wearing a collar with *her* man's name on it.

Her hands thrust forward before she thought about it, magic shooting from her fingertips in arcs of green lightning. The hit lifted Jezebel from her feet and sent her flying backward down the hall.

"For fuck's sake!" Max's head whipped toward Victoria, revealing a thunderous scowl. "Have you lost your mind?"

"Obviously *you* did when you brought that trash into my house!" she shot back, her hands fisting against the urge to strike out again.

A Mack truck slammed into her chest. At least that's what it felt like. She was tossed onto her back and sent skidding into the sofa. Victoria screamed, her chest smarting and pajama top smoking from the direct hit.

"Stop!" Max roared, stepping into the middle of the hallway as a barrier.

Jezebel pounced and leaped over him, spinning midair to land on her feet, her hair flowing around her like a cape. Victoria was even more nimble, her catlike reflexes kicking in with a vengeance. Max lunged, his arms wrapping around the witch from the back, and *poof.* They were gone.

Unreasonable fury coursed through Victoria along with a rush of magic the likes of which she'd never felt before. She trusted Max, believed in him, was sane enough to know he couldn't come at her the way he had all evening if he'd gotten off earlier with someone else.

That didn't mean she wasn't spitting mad that he'd brought his ex into their house, an ex who was bat-shit crazy and hurting for an ass kicking.

"Max!" she yelled. But he was gone.

Seething, she powered off the stereo and stalked through the house, searching for any trace of Jezebel. The rage grew when she found her and Max's bed mussed and smelling like the witch's perfume. It smelled like something else, too. Something smoky and slightly acrid. She tore off the sheets, shredding them with claws she hadn't realized had extended.

She was running through all the things she had to say to

Max when he returned, growing angrier with every minute that passed, when the wards around the apartment jingled with warning.

"You want more, witch?" she muttered, dropping the sheets and heading toward the door. Her palms started itching again, reminding her of the shot she'd taken before. Her magic had never manifested as lightning arcs of power previously. She needed Max to help her understand that. And a clearer head.

Gods, how much had this hunt affected them?

She reached the front door and realized the threat was behind her. The hairs on her nape stood on end and she pivoted, shifting to her feline form to make less of a target. The windows crackled with the energy surging from outside, and she shook off the clothes that were puddled around her paws and raced to one, leaping onto a console table to get a better look.

Eyes darting, she searched the skyline, seeing nothing to combat but feeling the pull of magic. It pierced her chest where the wound still throbbed, forcing a shift into a human form against her will. She fell from the console, back arching, magic flaring in a surge of power that shattered the windows.

A black cloud poured through the breach and solidified beside her as a man. Copper-haired, with eyes so dark they appeared black, he radiated a dark power that sent goose bumps racing across her bare flesh.

He knelt beside her and she found she couldn't move, could barely breathe. The place on her chest where Jezebel had struck her with magic burned as if she'd been hit with acid. It ate through her in agonizing darts, spreading throughout her body.

He smiled. "Relax. It won't last long."

The pain hit her heart and she cried out, her muscles seizing. Then she mercifully lost consciousness.

The moment Max materialized in Jezebel's home, he shoved her away from him, his palms burning from the touch of her skin. She was feverishly hot, her eyes wild. The deep gash by her shoulder from Victoria's strike didn't seem to register at all. And the curve of her lips was so crazed it gave him chills.

He waved a hand to clothe her in a robe.

"Max." She shook her head. "You didn't used to be this uptight. Clearly your Familiar isn't keeping you happy."

"You don't want to make an enemy out of me, Jezebel," he warned. "I suggest you think of me as a fond memory and stay the hell away."

"But we're drawn to each other! I know you feel it, too." She stepped closer, her hand extended as if to touch him.

And he did feel it. Enough to take a sharply indrawn breath. The call of like to like was strong, but it wasn't sexual. It was magical.

He met her halfway and yanked aside the material covering her wound. The motion bared her breast and made her gasp with excitement, but his attention was solely on the gash in her flesh that didn't bleed and was dark not because it was cauterized but because her blood was tainted.

"When did he get to you?" he demanded. "What did he do to you?"

Her hands slid up his chest. "I'm more interested in what *you're* going to do to me," she crooned.

Catching her wandering hands, he bridged the distance to the High Council. He took her directly to the antechamber outside the receiving hall. The room was crowded, as usual, and his sudden appearance with the half-naked Jezebel brought conversation and movement grinding to a halt.

The crowd of warlocks and witches parted for him as he strode forward to the desk where requests for an audience were logged, his hand at Jezebel's elbow driving her forward.

"She's been compromised by Xander Barnes," he said coldly. "She'll need treatment and rehabilitation."

He released her and moved to turn away.

"The Council will want to question you," the clerk said quickly.

"I don't know what happened, I wasn't there." Abruptly, Max recoiled, lurching back as white-hot agony pierced his chest like a blade. He felt a scream reverberate inside him and his blood ran cold.

"Victoria," he breathed, panic tearing through him.

Distracted and caught off guard, he'd left her alone and un-protected. He surged forward, transferring in midstep. It was like swimming in honey, his magic siphoning away from him with every beat of his heart. He tumbled back into his living room endless moments later, landing on his hands and knees in a mess of broken glass, disoriented and dazed.

Black leather heeled boots appeared in his vision, drawing his eye upward along mile-long legs capped with tight black shorts and a leather bustier. Victoria set her hands on her hips, her red-stained lips curving in a humorless smile. The emerald of her kohl-rimmed eyes was as dark as her aura.

"Now this," she purred, "is exactly how I want you."

Nine

He's taming you. And you're letting him.

Victoria watched Max push to his feet in a powerfully grace-ful movement, his stormy eyes assessing her. She knew he was wondering how to get the upper hand, but she wasn't open to playing those games anymore. She was more powerful than he was now and it was time he acknowledged it. The inequal-ity in their relationship—if they were going to have one—had shifted in her favor.

You have magic of your own, but he doesn't respect it.

"Victoria . . ."

She saw blood on his hands from the shattered window glass. Absently, she healed the cuts with a spell she'd never used before but inexplicably knew by heart.

You've made him more powerful than ever and how does he repay you? By subjugating you and making you subservient.

Her hand whipped out and caught his tie, and a moment later they were back in his loft.

His chest lifted and fell on a deep breath. "What did he do to you, kitten?" he asked softly.

"I'm not in the mood to talk, Max," she said, licking her lips at all the prospects his toy collection presented. *If he really loved you, he'd let you both play.* "I want to play."

"Do you?" He caught her face in his hands, studying her. "You can fight it off, sweetheart. Let me help you."

"You can help me now," she said, parroting what he'd said to her earlier. *Why should he get to have all the fun?* "I've wanted you tied to a bed since the first night we met."

"That's not how things work, Victoria. Not between warlock and Familiar, and certainly not between us. This isn't you talking."

"But it is!" She wrenched away from him. *You should listen to your instincts, Victoria St. John, they're telling you what you already know.* "You've been trying to change me since we met. You want me to be something I'm not!"

His jaw tightened. "We've been together almost two years. You don't strike me as the type of woman to put up with a man that long if he wasn't pleasing you."

"That was before." *Remember who you were before Westin hunted you down. Remember the power you had. The High Council let Darius Whitacre die. Did you ever make them pay for that? Have you used Westin the way he's used you?*

"Before what?"

"Before I saw what you really want!" She turned her back to him. "Jezebel was a real eye-opener for me."

Max could picture his kitten's tail swishing restlessly. He

didn't have to picture the darkness of her aura; he could almost taste it in the air. "I want *you.*"

She looked over her shoulder at him, as sly as a cat. "You can have me . . . if you're a good boy, Max."

He changed tactics. "All right. Let's catch up with Xander Barnes first. We deal with him, then we've got all the time in the world."

Tossing her head back, she laughed and walked toward the wall displaying his selection of floggers and crops. *"Now* you want me to hunt with you? After I practically begged you?"

Max shoved a hand through his hair, frustrated by his own contribution to the disaster he faced. He'd left Victoria wide open magically, physically, and emotionally. Even when they'd first met, they'd never been this far apart. He couldn't stand it.

He also couldn't let it affect his judgment. Hunters who allowed emotion to overrule reason were doomed to failure and he couldn't fail in this.

"I make mistakes, Victoria," he conceded. "In this case, I underestimated how much I need your help. And I underestimated Powell."

She walked to the chest of drawers where he kept the toys he put inside her. "Don't blame our problems on your hunt."

"I seem to have lost something in translation, then. Why don't you remind me what happened today? What's the last thing you remember before I came home?"

"I remember your mistress making herself at home in my house! Wearing a damned collar with your name on it!"

"And how did you get from that to where we are now?" With her dressed in an over-the-top dominatrix outfit he hadn't known she owned. Then again, he hadn't bothered re-

searching how things had gone with her and the Hunters previously assigned to collar her.

But even jealousy couldn't make his dick stop throbbing as
he looked at her. Despite everything that had gone wrong—or
maybe because of it and his desperate need to reconnect—he
was achingly attracted to this new side of her.

She pulled a glass dildo out of a drawer and ran her fingers
up and down the length of it. Then she lifted it to her lips and
licked the tip. Max bit back a groan.

"I realized I should start out the way I mean to go on," she
said, looking at him from beneath spiked lashes. "Relation-
ships go both ways, Max."

"I've given you everything I've got." He reached out with
his magic and slammed into the wall of power radiating off
her. She was siphoning from him by the moment, an irrefutable sign that she'd been tainted by black magic. "And I'll keep
giving it until I draw my last breath."

"Everything except your submission."

"I'm not a switch, kitten."

Her foot tapped a rapid staccato against the cement.
"Maybe I am. Does that mean we're incompatible?"

"You didn't think so an hour ago."

She narrowed her gaze at him, then disappeared, winking
away before his eyes.

"Victoria!" he shouted, his fists clenching.

It was diabolically clever what Barnes had done, taking away
Max's anchor while she was still breathing. Death would've
been more merciful than losing her to black magic. And he
couldn't take her to the Council as he had Jezebel, not just
because he was weakened to a dangerously low state, but be-

cause he feared they would vanquish her to mitigate any threat he might be perceived to be.

He racked his mind for options, trying to narrow down what spells Barnes might have used to turn Jezebel and Victoria.

"Blood magic," he muttered, knowing how powerful it could be.

But only as long as Barnes was alive.

Is Westin really the right man for you? Or is there someone out there who would suit you better?

Victoria hit the clubs. Restless and driven by urges she couldn't fight, she prowled the city searching for something she couldn't put her finger on. It irritated her that she felt the need to return to Max. A driving, spurring need. She'd never felt so torn before, as if she was warring with herself.

"Looks like you're in the mood to play, gorgeous."

She turned her head toward the man speaking to her. He was tall and fit, sandy-haired and mischievous-eyed. Her gaze raked him from head to toe, as did her magic. He was human.

Her mouth curved, her thoughts turning to how much fun it would be to dominate such a strapping male. It had been far too long since she'd been allowed to take the reins.

"Are *you* in the mood to play?" she purred.

"Always. Can I buy you a drink?"

She shook her head, debating where to take him. Max's place would be ideal, but she ruled it out. Her apartment was an option, especially since Max had seen fit to take his *ex*-mistress there. But an unwelcome and unwarranted stab of guilt held her back.

Damn it.

"Let's go somewhere," she said, deciding it was best to leave the decision to him. Maybe he had his own toys.

He grinned and thrust out his hand. "Steve. Feeling seriously lucky to have met you tonight."

"Victoria." Her fingers brushed over his palm, but his touch lacked the heat and magical connection she'd come to feel with Max. A sense of hollowness grew in her belly. The club's music pounded out of the speakers, spurring customers to hook up. Couples and triples writhed against one another on the dance floor, flooding the air with the scent of arousal and pheromones, but she felt oddly disconnected.

"Come on, Vicky." He caught her hand before it fell to her side and linked their fingers together. "I've got a room around the corner."

Westin's got you under his spell, Victoria. Whitacre never controlled you like that.

She frowned as she allowed Steve to lead her through the crush to the exit. Listening to her conscience had never been more difficult. And Steve's use of the nickname "Vicky" only made things worse. Only Darius had ever called her that.

Max's voice echoed in her mind. *This isn't you talking.*

Her hand tightened on Steve's. The warlock had twisted her mind . . . made her confused. She'd never been more conflicted.

"Do you live in the city?" Steve asked when they stepped out onto the sidewalk.

"Yes." She'd moved in after Darius died, closer to the central hub of magic in the country, so that she would have greater opportunities to provoke the Council.

"I like it here," he went on, filling the void left by her short answer. "First-time trip for me. I'll have to thank my boss for suggesting this conference."

Forcing herself to focus on the man she was with, she said, "Maybe I'll have to thank him, too."

His eyes sparkled in the light of the streetlamps. "Do I have to ask if you'll be gentle with me?"

"Is that what you want?"

"No."

She smiled genuinely. "Good. I'm not sure I can be gentle tonight."

A ripple of desire moved through his big body. His skin heated to her touch. "Having one of those nights, sweetheart?"

Her nostrils flared, filling her senses with the scent of his lust and excitement. "Yeah . . . you could say that."

Ten

*M*ax hit the streets. Barnes would be sticking close by, knowing Max was vulnerable now in a way he'd never been before. This hunt had turned into a game for Barnes, one he was willing to risk capture for. Vanquishing Max wasn't going to stop the Council from coming after him; other Hunters would follow. It wouldn't even buy the warlock time, because Max was fairly certain the Council had already widened the hunt. They probably didn't trust him now, and Jezebel's susceptibility would raise further alarm.

Coming after Max was sport for Barnes, a chance to get a little piece of his own back after the years of incarceration he'd suffered.

Victoria, where are you?

He ruthlessly suppressed the urge to find her. It would be pointless while she was under the fog of blood magic. Whatever programming Barnes had given her would be impossible to break through while the warlock was living.

But he couldn't fight the fear for her. For *them,* as a couple, because there had been an opening for Barnes to exploit. All this time Max had believed it was simply a matter of acclimation that caused the resistance Victoria displayed occasionally. He'd assumed that at heart she was like all Familiars. But perhaps she was unique beyond the magic Darius had given her. Perhaps she truly needed to share control rather than give it up completely.

Could he be the man she needed if that were the case?

"Westin. You look so forlorn."

Stiffening, Max slowed and looked for his quarry. A wry smile twisted his mouth at the thought. Really, *he* was the one being hunted. "It's been a rough day."

Barnes stepped out of the shadows. He looked harmless enough on the surface, like a thirty-year-old man out for a stroll, but dark power poured off him, buffeting Max with such fury it nearly sent him stumbling back a step. "That's too bad. It's been a great day for me."

Max nodded. "You wanted Powell dead."

"He would've become a liability eventually," Barnes said with a shrug. He dressed better these days. When Max first caught him, he'd been a thug. Now he wore tailored slacks and shirt, with polished oxfords and tie. "And he was stupid enough to think he was smarter than me."

"I underestimated you, too."

Barnes liked that. He grinned. "I was hoping you'd be more of a challenge."

"I'm sorry to disappoint." Max tried to tap into Victoria, to tug at least a little of his magic back, but there was nothing on the other end of their connection. It was as if it'd been severed completely.

An old man walking his Chihuahua passed them, giving them a wide berth and suspicious eye. The dog began yipping at Barnes and tugging at its leash, baring its teeth at the warlock. Barnes crouched and smiled. The dog whined and pissed itself.

"Remy!" the old man scolded. "Bad dog. Come on."

The warlock stood, laughing. "The world is full of pathetic creatures, isn't it, Westin?"

"Scaring small dogs should be beneath you," Max said, allowing the wand tucked into the sleeve of his shirt to slide out and into his palm. It was a child's learning tool, one he hadn't used in centuries, and only briefly then. Serving only to help focus magic in the training stage, it bore no power itself, but Max needed all the help he could get. He'd used the bulk of the magic he had left to reach out to the Transcendual Realm for help.

He wasn't the only one who loved Victoria and would do anything to keep her safe.

"Nothing is beneath me. That's why I'm as powerful as I am today." Barnes scrubbed a hand over his jaw. "Putting rules on magic is where the Council went wrong. Magic is *alive,* it breathes. Caging it is a crime."

"You don't give a shit about magic. It's power you want. You're drunk with it."

"I don't think you'd sound so disdainful if you still had yours," Barnes goaded, his gaze hard.

"And I don't think you'd sound so smug if you knew that the Council was about to hunt me Themselves, because They believe Victoria made me too powerful. If I were you, I would've considered that a better punishment than this. An eye for an eye. Instead, you're doing Them a favor."

Barnes *didn't* like that. His smile faded. "You must have a death wish, Westin."

"Maybe." He played up his vulnerability. "I don't want to live without Victoria and you've taken her away from me. So it's either you or me, Barnes."

"Well, I think we both know how that's going to end."

Max thrust out his hand, sending magic racing along the length of the wand to strike Barnes in the chest. The warlock stumbled back, spinning, but quickly righted himself and fired back.

The weight of the blow lifted Max off his feet and sent him flying several feet. Winded and in terrible pain, he curled in on himself, making as small a target as possible. The next blow of magic seized his heart and lungs, blackening his vision. His surroundings dimmed and roaring filled his ears. The next strike would kill him.

Victoria . . . His eyes squeezed shut as agony twisted his body. How would she survive losing two warlocks she loved? *Be safe, kitten,* he whispered to her. *I love you.*

"Here we are," Steve said, stopping in front of an InterContinental hotel. Setting his hand at the small of Victoria's back, he urged her through the revolving doors in front of him.

I didn't leave you with Westin for this, Vicky.

She came to an abrupt halt and the door smacked into her from behind, shoving her forward. She stumbled into Steve.

Darius? she breathed, astonished to hear the beloved voice again.

You told me you loved him . . . that you wanted to be with him. If you've changed your mind, darling, I'll bring you to me. Damned if I'll leave you to someone else.

"Easy," Steve said, taking the opportunity to run his hands down her back. "You all right?"

She shook her head. No, she was far from all right. A sick feeling of dread permeated her senses. She opened her mouth to tell him she'd changed her mind—

Pain sliced through her, causing her to arch her back and to press herself tight against Steve.

Be safe, kitten. I love you.

Terror filled her. *Max!*

For an instant she could see clearly, as if thick fog had momentarily blown aside, affording her a clear view.

Max was dying. And her heart was breaking.

Barnes screamed, a sound of fury and pain. Glass shattered nearby. Max felt magic coil tightly around them, then explode with resonating force. A woman cried out, a man cursed. Footsteps pounded by Max's head.

Power surged into Max with the force of a tornado, shoving out the pain and kick-starting his organs. He pushed upright, catching sight of Masters crouched beside him and firing volleys so quickly Max couldn't register them all. But Barnes was shielded by black magic, shrouded by undulating shadows that protected him from the relentless attack. Impressed and deeply grateful that the other Hunter had responded to the message Max left him, Max gathered the magic flowing through him and prepared to join the fray.

Victoria's aura pulsed through him. Power cycled from her, a raging circle that gathered strength with every pass. It was dark and smoky, more black than white, and its potency was so fierce it felt as if his skin was burning in an effort to contain it. Wind swirled around him, only him, his hair whipping with its fury. Power swelled inside him.

He saw her. She stood behind Barnes, her eyes glowing in the night, her arms lifted and extended, waiting for Max to strike so she could augment his power. Her legs were wide-spread and anchored to the cement, her beautiful features as cold and determined as he'd ever seen them. Ready to kill.

Barnes fired at Max with such force the hit rattled his bones, but he stayed upright and unharmed, fortified by his fury. Victoria had come for him, but she wasn't the same. He didn't know if she ever would be now that she'd been so thoroughly tainted. He didn't know if she had come back to him forever or just for now.

All he knew was that Barnes had to die.

Masters shouted as a hit knocked him back, rolling him end over end. Max fired. The ball of magic penetrated the shroud around Barnes and sent him back a shaky step . . . straight into an arc of lightning from Victoria that had him howling in angered pain. Pivoting, the warlock lurched toward her. Max moved, running forward and attacking. Masters appeared to his left, firing at the warlock's flank. The triple blow was irrecoverable.

Barnes exploded in a burst of black light, rattling the buildings around them and exploding the streetlights. Inky darkness descended, blocking out all light.

Victoria screamed his name and Max shouted in reply. He lunged toward the sound of her voice, moving by instinct, grunting when her slender body collided with his.

He whisked them away, leaving everything behind.

Epilogue

Victoria stared out the massive windows at the endless miles of snow that stretched out before her. The house sat high atop a mountain in one of the remotest parts of the world, hidden from the view of human eyes and satellite monitoring.

A week had passed since the night she'd helped Max and Gabriel vanquish Xander Barnes. She'd had no contact with anyone, not even the warlock who shared the home with her. He was there, so close. So gorgeous. So silent. He waited like the crafty Hunter he was. Waited and watched, his silver eyes following nearly every move she made. At night, he slept in a different room. A different bed.

As the hours crawled by, she felt more and more like herself. Her craving for Max grew by the day until it became a gnawing hunger she had trouble resisting.

His tendency to walk around wearing nothing but low-slung pajama bottoms didn't help.

But things were different now. *She* was different now. While the compulsion Barnes had programmed her with was gone, the taint of black magic remained and it freed a desire of a different sort. When she and Max made love, she lost herself in his touch . . . his hunger. At least once, she wanted to take him on her terms. To show him the depth of her love in some way other than through her submission.

But he wasn't a switch and the ease they'd once felt together was gone, leaving behind a wariness that made it difficult for her to reach out to him.

At least in her human form.

Shifting, she dropped to the floor and extricated herself from the folds of her maxi dress. She searched for him, allowing her animal instincts to guide her. There had to be a way for them to find a comfortable middle ground. If they could just work it out together . . .

She padded down the hallway, passing her room and finding his empty. She hurried on, exploring, her curiosity piqued for the first time in several days. The house remained a mystery to her after she'd spent so long just trying to get her head on straight. She'd slept, ate when Max cooked, and lay on the sofa watching television without really paying attention. It was like waking up after a long nap, fighting the grogginess that came with rejoining reality.

Reaching the end of the hall, Victoria spotted a half-opened door. She slowed and sniffed, purring when she smelled the darkly seductive scent of her warlock's skin. She pushed the door open with an uplifted paw, sitting as it swung silently open.

Max stood near the far wall, his back flexing as he reached

up and placed a crop in its holder above the fireplace, his inky hair brushing his shoulder blades.

"Hello, kitten," he said in that deep, rough voice she loved and had missed hearing.

He turned to face her and she drank him in, her gaze sliding over his powerful shoulders, firm pecs, and deeply ridged abdomen. Below the tie of his drawstring, his cock hung thick and heavy between his muscled thighs. Her purrs increased in volume. Her tail swished with anticipation.

A massive bed waited to the right, while the opposite wall displayed a vast collection of floggers, crops, and implements of bondage above the mantel. Two chests waited at the foot of the wide bed—one white, the other black. The white one had her name inscribed across the lid, while the other bore his. A Saint Andrew's cross was affixed to the wall, near a bondage chair and swing suspended from one of the wide beams in the ceiling. Light poured in from skylights above, as well as the wall of curtainless windows behind the bed.

She shifted. His breath caught at her nakedness and relief shimmered through her. He still wanted her.

"Max," she said, her voice husky with want.

He crossed his arms, teasing her with the sight of chiseled biceps. He was so strong, and yet even in the extremes of his lust, he never hurt her.

Still, he waited.

She swallowed hard. "Are we rogue?"

"We're as good as dead. If we lay low, I doubt they'll hunt us. But you'd have to give up everything. Everything you own. Everything you've worked for."

"Do I have to give *you* up?"

His throat worked, the only sign that he wasn't as calm as he appeared. "I hope you don't. I hope you'll give me a chance to . . . adjust."

Victoria stepped closer. "You'd do that for me?"

His gaze heated, grew tender. "I would do anything for you."

"My needs are different from yours, Max," she explained gently. "I want you bound sometimes. I want to pleasure you without losing my head over what you're doing to me. I want your surrender, but I don't want you submissive."

His chest expanded on a deep, slow breath. "It's hard for me, Victoria, needing you this much. Loving you is both the easiest and hardest thing I've ever done."

"You think I'm not scared? Especially now." She looked out the windows at the ceaseless stretch of white. "Being a Hunter isn't just what you do, it's who you are. I'm not sure I can be what you need when I'm the only thing you've got. If that makes any sense at all."

"Kitten, life with you will never be boring." Max came to her and wrapped his big hands around her throat, like the collar she wore. "Aside from the games we'll play in this room, we've got a lot to figure out magically. Masters was right. You and me, we're a unique pairing, and we've never really explored that, let alone exploited it. Who knows what we're capable of?"

"We're more gray than white now," she said, gripping his wrists. "And when I'm topping you and you're coming for me, the magic might—"

"I always come for you, regardless of who's on top."

He pressed his mouth to hers and she relaxed, pushing her worries out of her mind. They had this. They had each other. The rest would work itself out.

She kissed him back, her lips curving with love into a catlike smile.

SYLVIA DAY is the #1 *New York Times* and #1 internationally bestselling author of more than a dozen award-winning novels sold in forty countries. She is a #1 bestselling author in twenty countries, and a reader favorite across several genres with millions of copies of her books in print. Her Crossfire series has sold more than twelve million copies since its debut last year. Day has been nominated for the Goodreads Choice Award for Best Author and her work has been honored as Amazon's Best of the Year in Romance. She has won the *RT Book Reviews* Reviewers' Choice Award and been nominated twice for Romance Writers of America's prestigious RITA award. She is currently president of the Romance Writers of America, an association of more than ten thousand writers. Visit her at www.sylviaday.com and Facebook.com/AuthorSylviaDay. Follow Sylvia on Twitter @SylDay.

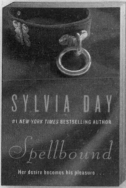